MURDER ON THE FLYING SCOTSMAN

A LADY THEA MYSTERY: BOOK 1

JESSICA BAKER

Book One of *A Lady Thea Mystery*.

Copyright © 2020 Jessica Cobine.

First Edition: March 2020.

ISBN: 978-1-7347202-0-4 (paperback)
ISBN: 978-1-7347202-1-1 (e-book)

Published 2020 by Jessica Cobine.

ACKNOWLEDGMENTS

I'd like to thank my parents
for supporting and believing in me.

CHAPTER ONE

1910 – Lady Theodora Prescott-Pryce crossed the platform of King's Cross Station as the trains rolled in with puffs of steam and smoke. Her bags had already been loaded, but she didn't want to get on her train before she had to. She would be trapped for nine hours from London with the same dull people, though the sacrifice was worth it to see her cousins in Scotland.

Her nerves had very little to do with the journey itself. It was the people she'd be stuck with, all of them ready to interrogate her. She was a young, unmarried woman, traveling only with her maid. The train was sure to be full of dowagers wondering why she wasn't engaged or married.

The masses swarmed towards their trains. They were making their final mad dash to board and find their seats before the train left without them. Most people were excited to take the train on a journey somewhere far away.

Thea spared a glance back at the clock. She had a few minutes before she needed to board. The hordes of people on the platform were overwhelming as she looked around, but she'd wait a little bit longer. Where was Molly?

She was mostly surprised that her maid hadn't tried to rush her to get on. It was so unlike Molly to be running late. Despite only being twenty, Molly Forbes had the oldest soul of anyone Thea had ever met. That included her grandmother who didn't believe in electricity or telephones and was thoroughly offended that Thea's American mother did.

At least this train wasn't taking her to Astermore to visit her brother. If that were the case, then she would have been obligated to visit her grandmother. She didn't dislike seeing her grandmother, but she always felt like she was a disappointment after visiting her. The Dowager Countess Prudentia Prescott-Pryce felt that all women should be married or engaged before the end of their first Season, like she had been, that they should be mothers before they had passed three Seasons.

Thea didn't want to get married so young. To do so, she would give up her freedom. At twenty-two, she was independently wealthy thanks to her American aunt Dorothea. The Season was just an endless parade of parties and balls. Once she married, she and her money would be under her husband's thumb. It would put an end to her lifestyle as she knew it.

A stern-faced woman in a navy suit dragged a girl only a few years younger than Thea. Blonde-haired and blue-eyed, the girl would have no trouble finding a husband based on her looks, although her clothes were expensive but ill-fitting, as if they had been made for someone else.

The girl's heel caught on one of the cracks in the platform and she stumbled. Immediately, her mother turned to scold her. The girl looked to be on the verge of tears, but her mother didn't seem to care. Thea didn't envy that girl at all.

She glanced back at the clock. Where was Molly? It was quite unlike her to disappear for so long. Her maid had claimed she was only going to the lavatory. Thea was going to head there to see what happened to her when she noticed a man in a tan coat staring at her. There was nothing particularly special about him, other than she felt as if he were watching her. He had a thoughtful expression on his face, like he had seen her somewhere before and was trying to place where he knew her from. He looked vaguely familiar, though she would puzzle over trying to place him.

She was yanked from her thoughts by an older man ramming his trolley into her side. He apologized profusely, but Thea barely heard him. The man in the coat had vanished into thin air.

Thea shivered and fiddled with her purse to occupy her hands.

It was then, from the smoke, that Molly materialized beside her. "I beg your pardon, my lady. I didn't mean to be gone so long."

Molly almost looked older than she was. She had her long brown hair tied back into a tight, proper chignon. She wore a dark gray walking suit, one of Thea's castoffs. It was an older style, but Molly wore it rather well. The boots were her own, just plain black, no frills.

Thea studied her maid. Her eyes were red-rimmed, and she kept looking over her shoulder, eyes darting nervously around the station. Something or someone had upset her.

"My lady, please, we need to get going," Molly begged, throwing an anxious look behind in the direction of the clock.

Thea nodded.

The conductor was a short, portly man with an over-waxed mustache. Molly followed half a step behind, as if she was expecting to have to push Thea onto the train. Thea could barely keep from rolling her eyes at her maid.

He took their tickets, smiling at both of them as they boarded the car which contained their compartment. Crowds made traveling difficult for her. Thea wasn't sure why but being under the eyes of so many judgmental people had always made her nervous. Traveling by train would not be so bad if it weren't for the forced interactions between the other passengers any time she left the compartment. She almost dreaded going to dine, since the restaurant car always seemed filled with the same busybodies. After three unsuccessful Seasons, she would have thought she would have been used to it, but it felt like they were waiting for her to make a mistake.

Passengers shuffled through the tight corridor. Once they reached her compartment, Thea collapsed onto the bench. She had always loved being in the more public cars when she had traveled as a child. Now that she had grown and was an unmarried, mostly unchaperoned woman, the disapproving glares from the matrons had her cowering away in her compartment.

She reached up and pulled the pin from her hat, sighing in relief as the heavy weight was removed from her head. Instantly, Molly rushed to take it from her hands. Thea opened the buttons on her jacket and despite her corset, she felt as if she could actually breathe again.

The train whistled loudly, the shrill noise piercing the air before the car jolted forward. The view outside the window shifted as the train pulled from the station. The wheels clicked on the track. Steam surged up, obstructing her view.

"Shall I get you some water, my lady?" Molly asked softly, offering a small smile.

"No, thank you," Thea replied gratefully. She shrugged off her jacket, laying it on the seat beside her.

Molly was ruffling through her travel bag. She pulled out Thea's worn copy of *A Study in Scarlet* and opened the book. Thea smiled and shook her head as her maid buried her nose in the book. She wouldn't be surprised if the girl had brought as many books as she could fit in her satchel. Still, Thea found it funny how Molly disliked violence, but loved to read books about murder. Rather than read like Molly, she turned back to the window and watched as London began to pass them by.

Motorcars drove beside horse-drawn carriages on the cramped London streets. People from all walks of life rushed to and fro. Soot-covered children in tattered rags ran down cobbled streets. Women in their suffragette uniforms marched, their banners displayed proudly in protest. Stuffy businessmen watched the suffragettes with sneers on their faces, or so she imagined since she was too far to see them clearly.

As the city moved outside of her view, Thea's thoughts began to drift and fade away. She leaned her head against the wall beside the window. The world passed by as the train gently rocked. The constant clacking of the wheels on the track made her eyelids grow heavy.

CHAPTER TWO

THE SCRAPING OF THE COMPARTMENT DOOR PULLED THEA FROM her fitful sleep. She thought she heard the door latch shut and Molly's boots hit the floor.

"Daniel!" Molly exclaimed. Thea's brow furrowed, but she forced herself not to open her eyes. To the best of her knowledge, Molly didn't know any men named Daniel. "What are you doing? You can't be here. Not now."

"I needed to see you. It's important." Daniel's voice was desperate.

The rustle of clothing made Thea risk opening her eyes. Daniel was the man from the platform who had been wearing the trench coat. He swept Molly into his arms and kissed her soundly. Thea was sure she was dreaming. She had never seen two people kiss with so much passion, not outside of her imagination. It was like watching Shakespeare performed. It was so soft and gentle and all-consuming that she had to close her eyes because she felt as if her heart was being squeezed watching it.

Molly was the one who pulled away, but Daniel kept stroking her cheek. It was like he needed to reassure himself that she was still there. His eyes were fixed on her, like he feared she would disappear if he looked away.

Thea had a clear view of Daniel's face. He had been the man who had been watching her at the station. He was tall and handsome, with dark blond hair and bright eyes. He had removed the outer coat and was wearing a well-tailored suit.

"Why are you here, Daniel?" Molly asked softly.

"Please, Molly. I need your help." His voice trembled as he spoke. Thea had never heard a man sound like that before, almost terrified.

"You need to go." Thea squeezed her eyes shut as Molly started to turn around.

"I need you to take this." There was a sound like paper crumpling in his hands as it rustled against the fabric of his jacket. Thea fought against the instinct to look.

"Please go, Daniel, before she wakes up. I can't explain you being here."

"Just promise me you'll keep it safe for me until we reach Edinburgh. I'll explain everything there."

Thea opened her eyes again. Daniel's hands were closed over Molly's as he pushed something, maybe an envelope, into her hands. She couldn't see Molly's expression from her angle, but she imagined the girl was eying him suspiciously. "What is it?"

He shook his head. "Hopefully nothing important. But if anything happens to me, you need to give this to the police."

"Is this going to put me in danger?" He didn't answer, was silent for several minutes. "Daniel, are you in danger?"

"I hope not, my love." He dipped his head to kiss Molly. The girl tilted her head up to meet his lips. He muttered something against her skin, burying his face in her neck. The whole embrace was scandalous and yet so very tender and sweet. There was something about the way she clung to him, almost unwilling to let go that lent an air of tragedy to the whole affair.

Then, he pulled back and left her compartment as quickly as he could without making too much noise. Molly started to turn around towards her, but Thea shut her eyes. She didn't know if she had just imagined the entire thing or if it had really happened.

AN HOUR HAD TO HAVE PASSED BEFORE THEA WOKE UP AGAIN. Feeling drowsier than she had before her nap, she blinked and rubbed the sleep from her eyes. Molly was curled up on the opposite seat, her nose buried in the book. Looking at her, Thea would have never known that anything had happened while she had been asleep.

It was still bright outside, brighter than it had been before her nap. It seemed like the sun had risen to mid-sky.

Thea straightened up. Instantly, Molly sat up.

"Is there anything I can get for you, my lady?"

Thea shook her head as she stood and stretched. She caught a glimpse at the book Molly was so immersed in and smiled. She was still reading the same Sherlock Holmes novel. Molly was obsessed with a good mystery novel. "I'm alright." She glanced at her wristwatch. It was after one o'clock. She yawned a little, lifting her hand to cover her mouth. "I think I'll go for lunch. Have you eaten?"

"Yes, my lady. The trolley came around a little bit ago. I had a sandwich." Molly motioned to the cold, half-eaten sandwich that had been discarded on the seat. Thea grimaced. From the pallor of Molly's complexion, Thea doubted the food had tasted good.

"Would you care to join me in the restaurant car for a real meal?"

She knew Molly would decline. Molly always declined since she felt it was improper for her as a maid to dine with her employer in the restaurant car. But Thea's American mother had not raised her as primly as someone more British might have and so she had no qualms about asking Molly to eat with her, despite already knowing her response.

Molly shook her head. "No thank you, my lady." She blinked. "Unless you want me to join you, my lady?"

Thea smiled slightly as she shook her head. "No, stay. Enjoy your book."

Thea waited a moment until her maid relaxed into the seat and lifted the book back up to begin reading again. Thea exited her compartment and headed in the direction of the dining car. As she walked, she noticed a man coming towards her from the dining car. At first, she did not register his face, not until she brushed against him, their shoulders bumping. He turned and moved to the side to let her pass. It was Daniel, Molly's lover, she realized.

"Excuse me, miss," Daniel said softly.

Thea swallowed. It hadn't all been a dream. Up until that point, she hadn't been completely convinced otherwise.

He seemed to be pretending to not know who she was. Perhaps he didn't know her.

She thought she had imagined the whole thing. But a small flicker of recognition in his eyes told otherwise.

THE HEAD WAITER WAS STANDING IN A SMALL ALCOVE, JUST OFF the main corridor of the restaurant car. He wore the same sort of uniform as the waiters at the most fashionable restaurants in London. The head waiter inclined his head, respectfully.

"Are you dining alone this afternoon, Lady Theodora?" She was a bit surprised that he knew her name. She supposed that they had been told to learn each First-class passenger's name so they could greet them personally when they came in.

"Yes." She smiled at him.

"Right this way, my lady."

Thea nodded and followed him as he led her to a table for four. She took the seat closest to the window. It felt more open, as if she had an escape from the coming small talk. It was still early, so most of the car was empty. There were a few already seated, but no one she recognized from the society pages.

People trickled into the car, slowly at first, but before the waiter could bring her something to drink, there were only a handful of empty seats left. Thea glanced at the unoccupied chairs at her table. If she had truly wished to avoid interactions with the other passengers, she would have asked for one of the tables that only sat two people and insisted that Molly come along with her.

The head waiter returned. He led a portly gentleman with a waistcoat that was straining over his stomach. The man held himself stiffly, formally. If Thea was a betting woman, she'd say he was former military.

The man's clothing was made from expensive materials and his shoes were definitely not the shoes of an average middle-class man. He had graying hair. She'd say he was probably only a few years older than her father would have been, had he still been alive.

The man bowed slightly. "Allow me to introduce myself. I am Colonel Stephen Bantry. How do you do?"

"Good afternoon, Colonel Bantry. I am Lady Theodora Prescott-Pryce."

He pulled out a chair on the other side of the table by the aisle, facing the door. "I do hope you won't mind eating with an old bachelor like me, Lady Theodora."

"Not at all, Colonel."

"I'm afraid I'm not very good company."

She laughed awkwardly. "That's fine with me." He rewarded her with a pleasant smile. "You wouldn't happen to be the same Stephen Bantry who was the author of *Parvati*?"

The book had been one of her favorites. Her brother had given it to her one Christmas after a classmate's father brought it back from India. She had read the stories in it enough times to have them memorized, her copy tattered from years of enjoyment. In the book, he translated and adapted the Hindu legends of the goddess Parvati, whose love of Shiva endured through her rebirth.

The Colonel had served in British India for many years. In his autobiographical work about his life in India, he explained how he had come from a well-to-do family and had followed a school friend into the army. Thea had made a quest of finding his books. They had been hard to come by in England.

He grimaced. "I'm afraid so. You've read it then?"

"I found it fascinating."

She shifted slightly in her chair. Perhaps he would carry most of the conversation for her. What did one say when they met their favorite author?

The next person to join them was a woman who looked to be only a few years older than Thea. Her blonde, bouncing ringlets strained from her hairdo, threatening to break free at any moment. Her vivid-colored wardrobe seemed to match her personality. Her rich purple skirt was paired with a fashionably cut blue silk shirt. There was a certain air to the woman, like she glowed from the inside. There was an almost foreign quality to her that Thea couldn't quite put her finger on.

"Mrs. Livingston," she introduced herself, smiling largely at the waiter. "Thank you ever so much."

The waiter bowed his head, clearly uncomfortable with being thanked for doing his job. He departed and Mrs. Livingston's full attention came back to the table.

"How do you do?" the woman asked, eyes shimmering as

she offered her hand to Thea. Her accent was definitely not British. It was overdone, like she was an actor on the stage forcing her words to be said that way. She lowered herself into the seat next to Thea with that same overdramatic flare, every movement exaggerated. She batted her eyes at the Colonel with the same excessive manner as her accent.

The Colonel introduced them both to Mrs. Livingston before he leaned forward. "I couldn't help but notice your unusual accent. Where are you from, Mrs. Livingston?"

"Please, do call me Wilhelmina. Mrs. Livingston is so stiff." She shuddered. "I'm from Texas. My daddy is an oilman. When I was marryin' age, my mama packed us on up and brought me on over here."

Thea was having a hard time believing anything coming out of her mouth. Her story seemed too rehearsed, just like her accent. It felt scripted like Mrs. Livingston was just an actress on the stage, just like everything else about her. The Colonel smiled and nodded, but otherwise didn't comment. He clearly didn't believe her either.

It was strange to think of her as an American. Growing up, Thea had always thought of Americans as the quiet types like her mother or uncle or cousins. Her aunt hadn't been as restrained as her siblings, but since she had also raced automobiles, Thea had never thought Dorothea to be like anyone else.

She knew that couldn't have been the case for the entire country, because a quiet country did not start a war over every little thing. It seemed like any time she received a letter from her American cousins, their country was off to fight someone new.

Perhaps her mother had learned to be more British. That seemed more likely. She certainly didn't act like the overly liberated Mrs. Livingston.

Thea stayed silent, as usual. She hardly felt the need to

improve the silence with unnecessary small talk. Mrs. Livingston clearly disagreed with her.

"Well aren't ya'll just a talkative bunch?" she said.

Thea sighed and turned to the woman, picking the one topic that usually shut the mouths of women so clearly looking for a lover outside of their marriage. She had gathered a lot of experience in doing just that, usually when they questioned why she was still unmarried. "So will your husband be joining us for lunch?"

It seemed that Mrs. Livingston was the one woman in the entire world that this was untested on, as the method quickly proved itself untrue.

"Mr. Livingston had some business to attend to in London still. Such a shame that he'll be missing out. He'll be traveling up in a few days. These big house parties are to die for."

She smiled charmingly at the Colonel, who acted as if he were oblivious to her, smiling and nodding just so. Mrs. Livingston deflated when she saw that he wasn't taking her bait to start a conversation. Thea supposed that it couldn't be any fun trying to have a one-sided conversation, but she made no effort to join the discussion. Besides, she highly doubted the other woman's dejected mood would last for long.

The rest of the car was filling up. Thea wondered about who the next person was that the head waiter would bring over. Would they be reserved like the Colonel or loud and outspoken like Mrs. Livingston? She was hoping for someone more like the Colonel. She didn't think she could survive lunch with two people like Mrs. Livingston, both working in tandem to drive her into insanity.

To Thea's pleasant surprise, the head waiter led a young man, younger than Colonel Bantry, but older than Mrs. Livingston to the table. He was tall with soft brown curls that looked like you could run your fingers through them. She wouldn't call him handsome, but she could see how he could be considered attractive. His eyes were probably the most engaging part of his face to her. They seemed like they saw everything. When he caught her staring, a small smirk crossed over his face.

The Colonel stood, shaking the younger man's hand. "It has been some time."

"Yes, it has. I hope you are well."

"I am, thank you." The Colonel waved to Thea and Mrs. Livingston. "This is the Honorable Edward Thayne? Thayne, may I present Lady Theodora Prescott-Pryce and Mrs. Wilhelmina Livingston."

"A pleasure to meet you both," Mr. Thayne greeted, inclining his head to them.

Thea smiled. "It's nice to meet you, Mr. Thayne."

"How do you do, Mr. Thayne?" Mrs. Livingston asked, her intentions obvious in her voice as she looked up at him through her angelically long lashes.

Thea rolled her eyes and the Colonel chuckled. It seemed the newcomer had lifted the other woman's spirits again. Nothing seemed to be able to keep her down for long. She wasn't sure if that was a good or a bad thing.

"How do you do, Mrs. Livingston?" Mr. Thayne took the seat next to the Colonel, the only free one at the table. "Are you, by chance, related to Francis Livingston?"

Mrs. Livingston's smile faded away. "He's my brother-in-law."

He eyed her. "So you must be the American that Francis' older brother, Ernest, married?"

"Yes," Mrs. Livingston said stiffly.

"I'm sorry to have missed the wedding. I was unavailable that weekend."

"That's quite alright." Wilhelmina forced a smile, but quieted.

Mr. Thayne smiled at the rest of them as the waiter

brought over drinks and the first course. Thea felt a little warm inside as his gaze turned on her, like she had drunk a little too much champagne a little too fast.

Unable to look at him any longer, Thea dropped her gaze to her hands. She focused on pulling off her gloves and folding them neatly into her purse. They were her favorite pair of white gloves.

"So what brings ya'll on up to Scotland?" Mrs. Livingston had presented the question to the table, but it was spoken directly to Mr. Thayne. Like the Colonel, the younger man appeared to be oblivious or immune to her charms, preferring to watch the rest of the car rather than their table.

Thea bit her tongue. She wished Molly was eating with her. It was a shame since Molly made for very good company. Most of the time, her maid seemed far better suited for high society than Thea. Thea had often wondered if she could get away with switching places with the maid to rid herself of the social obligations.

Perhaps life would have been easier if she was as outgoing as Mrs. Livingston. She seemed to make friends easily. The woman certainly didn't care what people thought about her. She was larger than life. Mrs. Livingston made Thea's small acts of childhood rebellion look mild. Thea wondered what that would feel like, if it would be freeing?

She hated the trivialness of the socially acceptable meal topics, or worse yet, that they even had to converse over their food at all. Somehow, talking through her meal always seemed to take her appetite away. It appeared that was not the case for Mrs. Livingston.

"Colonel?" Mrs. Livingston started, when no one answered her question.

"An old army friend lives up there." He smiled. "I'm afraid you wouldn't find it very fascinating. Just a couple of old bachelors. Nothing terribly exciting."

She smiled blindingly at the older gentleman and reached a hand across the table to him. "I'm sure you'll have a lovely time all the same."

She actually sounded sincere, though Thea doubted she was. *How did she do it*, she marveled.

The other woman turned her attention on to Mr. Thayne. She stared at him, but the other man handled it admirably. He didn't even flinch, didn't so much as shift under the woman's gaze, though that could have been since he seemed to favor watching the other passengers.

"And you, Mr. Thayne?"

To his credit, Mr. Thayne didn't skip a beat.

"My family lives in Scotland. I haven't seen them in quite some time." It was a vague answer. Mr. Thayne didn't actually appear to be interested in the woman sitting next to Thea.

There was a woman across the aisle that caught Thea's attention. She was probably not much older than Thea, eating lunch with a man three times her age and seemed absolutely miserable. The woman's suit was a deep shade of burgundy red. It was a color Thea wished she could wear but it unfortunately washed out her skin, making her look pallid and sickly.

Besides the suit, the woman also sported a matching hat. It was a rather attractive hat, with large flowers and little fruit and shiny flecks of garnet. The woman kept glancing at her watch, as if this were the last place she wanted to be. Fortunately enough for Thea, Mrs. Livingston had taken it upon herself to entertain the table and so she was not in the same position as the woman across the aisle.

"Well that'll be a real treat." Mr. Thayne smirked at Mrs. Livingston as if there was some great joke that they hadn't been let in on. Finally, it seemed, it was her turn as the American woman turned on her. "And you, Lady Theodora?"

"The same." She thought back to her usual tricks for conversations. "What about you, Mrs. Livingston?"

"Some friends of Mr. Livingston are having a small gathering." Thea could hear pain in the other woman's voice. It was the first real emotion she had seen from the woman. Mrs. Livingston had seemed so cheerful, as fake as the rest of the society people Thea met. But the other woman didn't want to be going up there any more than Thea wanted to be making small talk. "He sent me on up here even though he couldn't attend."

Thea could hardly imagine being packed away like baggage and sent off to a party where you didn't even know or like anyone. It was clear that Mrs. Livingston didn't love her husband. It was painfully obvious that her husband didn't love her either.

Had Mrs. Livingston loved her husband at some point? It certainly seemed that way. Why else would she sound so hurt that he wasn't attending? That was just another reason to not get married. Thea could imagine few things worse than to be trapped in a loveless marriage like so many of her peers.

Mrs. Livingston pushed her food on the plate. She was swallowing hard and hadn't looked back up. Her eyes seemed a little too bright.

Thea pursed her lips. Her heart went out to the other woman. How awful to love someone who would never love you in return.

"Well that will be nice for you to see old friends," the Colonel said diplomatically, but Thea couldn't help but think that it was exactly the opposite of how Mrs. Livingston felt about her destination.

The other woman smiled, but it was more of a grimace, the look of someone being sent to their execution. She was saved by the first course being cleared and the second course being placed on the table before them.

Thea stared over at Mr. Thayne. He wasn't paying much attention to his food, but he was keeping more to himself than

Thea would have initially expected. There was something about him, how he kept glancing around, looking at the door, watching as if he expected something to happen. She turned her head quickly, looking behind her to see if there was anything she should be worried about.

Watching him was making her nervous. Her eyes scanned over the dining car, looking for someone of interest to watch, since the conversation at her own table had effectively died. Again, Thea found herself watching the woman across the aisle in burgundy. The woman had stood in a hurry and placed her napkin on the table. She made her excuses to the gentleman and rushed out. Thea frowned, wondering the story on that. She probably would never know it but was curious about it anyway.

Mrs. Livingston was watching the woman too with a slightly puzzled look on her face. She caught Thea's eye, but didn't say anything.

It wasn't until the meal was finished and all the courses had been cleared that the conversation started back up again.

"Well, it has been a pleasure, Lady Theodora, Mrs. Livingston, Mr. Thayne," the Colonel said, standing up from the table and pushing his chair in. He shook Mr. Thayne's hand and offered nods to both her and Mrs. Livingston.

"Please, I do believe we're all friends here. I insist you call me Wilhelmina," she drawled in her over-exaggerated accent, mostly to Mr. Thayne. Her smile looked fake to Thea's eyes.

"You make me feel like a young man again, Wilhelmina," the older man said amiably. He left the table and walked out of the restaurant car. Mrs. Livingston smiled and giggled girlishly, though this seemed to be as much of an act as her attempts at conversation.

"I do think it's time to take my leave. It was a real pleasure to meet ya'll. I do hope we'll be seeing each other again." Although the way she was batting her eyes, it was very clear who she wanted to see. She all but thrust her hand into his face.

"Of course, Mrs. Livingston," Mr. Thayne said amused, purposely ignoring her statement about calling her Wilhelmina. He took her offered hand. When she was out of earshot, he turned his charming gaze on her. "And you, Lady Theodora?" he inquired, "Will you too be leaving the table now?"

"No, Mr. Thayne. I think I'll be staying for a few moments."

This seemed to please him, and Thea found she didn't mind too much. He wasn't bad company. He had been quiet and polite.

"Well, I do believe we're friends now, according to Mrs. Livingston," Thea tried to joke. He was silent for a moment and her stomach twisted. This was why she didn't do well with people. She never knew the right thing to say. But then, he laughed loudly. As if realizing that it wasn't proper, he pressed his lips together tightly, lifting his napkin to cover his mouth. But his eyes were still twinkling as he spoke.

"I must say, I prefer to be called Leslie," he grinned, "since we are friends now."

"Then it's Thea."

"Well then, *Lady* Thea," he said, his eyes sparkling in amusement, "it's a pleasure to make your acquaintance."

The man sitting across from her at the table was charismatic, but awkwardly so. She narrowed her eyes at him.

"Leslie, not Edward?"

"My uncle's name is also Edward. He lived with us, so it was always confusing who was being called." Thea nodded, but didn't say anything. "My mother's cousin is the Earl of Rothes, so I was the lucky son to get her name. Everyone at home used to call me that and it stuck."

She laughed. "I'm named after my aunt too. My mother

thought she was being clever with Theodora because her sister was Dorothea."

Mr. Thayne chuckled. "At least it's better than my brother. He was named after our grandmother. Her name was Cathcart."

Thea grinned at that, but they both fell silent. She tugged on the sleeve of her blouse. She wasn't charming like Mrs. Livingston, wasn't able to come up with conversation so easily. There was something about him, something she couldn't put her finger on, something she wanted to know more about. He was too observant, too aware of his surroundings. Most gentlemen of her class were too absorbed in their own lives to pay attention to the world around them.

"Have you been up to Scotland before?" he asked finally. Thea knew only his name and that he was the son of Baron Thayne and was going up home to visit his family.

The woman in burgundy who had left in such a rush earlier was coming back to her table. Thea might not have paid the woman any more attention, if she hadn't left in such a strange manner in the middle of the meal. Rolling her wrist around so she could glance at her watch, Thea realized the woman had been missing for nearly thirty minutes.

It was curious that the woman had slipped back in as if she had always been there despite missing the entire meal. The woman had changed out of her suit into a simple dark dress, the color of burgundy wine. It was something very peculiar about all of it.

"Hmm?" she questioned when she realized Mr. Thayne was still staring at her expectantly. She blinked, trying to remember what it was he had asked. Had she been to Scotland before? "Oh yes, several times," she muttered distractedly as she resumed picking at her sleeve as she watched the woman resume her lunch.

Mr. Thayne frowned, glancing back quickly across the aisle to see who or what she was watching. "What is it?"

"Nothing," she lied. Mostly, it was just a general sense that something wasn't quite right, but Thea couldn't place her finger on it. There was nothing strange about a woman changing her clothing, Thea told herself.

Maybe the woman had spilt something on her suit, she speculated. That would explain why the woman had been in such a rush. She didn't want to be embarrassed by whatever had been on it. But it seemed strange that it would take so long to change clothes.

Thea shook her head, trying to clear it. It was just speculation. It wasn't important and she doubted she would ever know.

CHAPTER THREE

THEA STUCK THE KEY IN HER COMPARTMENT DOOR AFTER SHE had retreated from the restaurant car. Mr. Thayne had been lovely. He had offered to walk her back to her compartment, but she hadn't wanted to wait.

The key stuck, turning but not allowing the door to open. She glanced down, wondering why the door would be giving her such trouble. That was when she saw it. There was part of a bloodied boot print on the ground outside her door.

Swallowing the lump in her throat, her first thought was of Molly. Molly had fallen as the train bounced. The girl had hit her head inside the compartment and was now slumped against the door. It would explain why the door was giving her such a hard time, but not the bloodied boot print.

Thea crouched in front of the boot print. It appeared to have a high heel, a woman's shoe maybe. Why was there a woman's shoe print outside her door?

Thea slid the door open and nearly screamed in shock at the sight on the other side. Of all the things she had prepared herself to see, this was not one of them.

Molly was nowhere to be seen. Instead, a man lay face

down on the floor in her compartment. He had one arm stretched out to the bench as if he had been trying to reach something, his fingers and nails covered in blood.

"Excuse me," she said. The man didn't respond, so she leaned down closer, figuring he might be unconscious. "I said, excuse me, sir."

There was still no response from the man. In the back of her mind, Thea knew the man wasn't unconscious. He was too still.

Thea reached out to him. His skin, while mostly warm even through her gloves, was cooler to the touch than anyone should be. She breathed in hard, preparing herself for the worst.

Thea pushed at the man's shoulder until she rolled his body over. He was completely limp. A large crimson stain had spread across his well-tailored shirt and in the center, there was a knife buried deep into his chest. The blood was still wet, and she had to be careful not to get it on her hands. She didn't succeed.

The second thing Thea noticed was that she had seen the man before. Daniel.

She inhaled sharply, feeling if there was any sort of pulse from him. When she found none, she stood up. Whoever had killed Daniel had to be still on the train, she assumed. There had been a struggle from the obvious state of his clothes, from the blood on his outstretched hand. What could he possibly have done to deserve to be killed in such a way?

Poor Molly, Thea couldn't help but think. The girl was going to be devastated.

Thea stared at the body for another moment before she did the only logical thing that someone in her position could do. She screamed as loudly as she possibly could, backing into the corridor as she did so. She didn't want to be near the body, didn't want anyone else to think she was involved with killing him. She had read enough mysteries where the police had blamed the first person with the body.

Molly came down the corridor. The girl stumbled as she reached the compartment, eyes wide as she took in Thea pressed against the wall.

"My lady, what's-?" Molly's words cut off the minute she saw the body on the floor. Whatever color was in her face drained. "Daniel!" she cried before she lunged forward. Thea barely got an arm around Molly's waist in time to stop her from flinging herself at his body.

Molly reached out to grasp the doorframe, using it to keep her upright. Her body swayed dangerously before the girl crumpled to the floor.

On hands and knees, Molly scrambled over to Daniel's body and clutched at his shirt. The girl shook the body as if that would somehow make him wake up. She pressed her hands around the wound, as if she could stop the bleeding, as if he was still alive.

"Daniel, please," she begged, "You need to wake up. Please."

Molly buried her face into Daniel's chest just above the knife as she sobbed. It was a heartbreaking scene, painful to witness. But Thea wasn't watching her.

There was something shiny in his other hand, metallic. It looked long and thin, like a hatpin. She moved, trying to get a better view of it and caught sight of what looked like a piece of a ruby beneath the blood.

Before Thea could get a better look, she realized that a crowd of other first-class passengers and attendants had gathered. They all seemed shocked, whispering and muttering amongst themselves.

Mr. Thayne pushed his way through the crowd with a wave of the object that he held in his hand. He peered around the doorway of her compartment, oddly composed for discovering two women with a dead body in their compartment. Thea didn't know why she found him to be a completely welcome sight.

Mr. Thayne turned to the gathering crowd, holding up the object in his hand and Thea caught a glimpse of his badge as he flashed it. "Ladies and gentlemen, I am Detective Inspector Thayne from Scotland Yard. I need someone to contact the police in York immediately."

"Yes, sir," one of the stewards answered and left.

"If the rest of you will just go to the parlor car. I'm sure the police will have questions for you once we reach York." He turned to a few of the attendants. "Will you escort them out?"

"Yes, sir!" the boy all but saluted, then went to work forcing the onlookers to disperse.

CHAPTER FOUR

THE CONDUCTOR AND THE STEWARDS GUIDED THE PASSENGERS towards the back cars away from the crime scene.

Thea watched as Inspector Thayne entered the compartment. He stood between Molly and Daniel, gently guiding the girl away from the body. Inspector Thayne didn't seem too concerned about the blood soaking her maid's shirt as he put his arm around her to firmly move her into the hallway.

Molly was in hysterics. The girl sobbed, her eyes red, and she seemed unsure what to do with her hands. Poor Molly, she had to be traumatized.

Thea stood pressed against the wall. She didn't move. She felt strangely detached from the poor girl's suffering.

"I need you to calm down," Inspector Thayne was saying gently to Molly, placing his hands on her maid's shoulders.

"Please," she begged, fighting to get back into the room, even as Inspector Thayne kept Molly in the hallway. Thea filed out behind them and stood next to the window, as out of the way as she could stay.

"I can't let you back in there." How was he so calm? Thea

envied him. She knew it wouldn't be long before she fell apart herself, but right now she felt so numb.

"But he's— I need to—" Molly gasped out, tears streaming down her face. She was just moments away from fainting. Thea swallowed deeply, unsure how to deal with such a thing.

"Miss," Inspector Thayne said with a gentleness that she envied. He pulled a handkerchief from his jacket and offered it to Molly. "That compartment is a crime scene."

"Daniel," she muttered miserably.

"You know the deceased?" Inspector Thayne asked clinically, though not uncaringly. His voice was soft, like he had dealt with this kind of thing before. He had to have years of practice to be a Detective Inspector from Scotland Yard. He probably had the most experience dealing with grieving women of anyone on the train.

What was Daniel doing in her compartment? Why would they kill him in her compartment? A lot of things didn't add up. But who was she to point that out to a police detective?

"Daniel," Molly whimpered, "His name is Daniel."

Inspector Thayne looked at the maid then glanced at Thea. She shrugged. Before today, she never had an inkling that Molly had known any man more than just in passing.

Thea wondered if she would be a suspect in Daniel's murder. Perhaps it was a good thing that she had eaten lunch in the dining car where she had been around other people.

But what about Molly? The maid had been supposedly alone in Thea's compartment. After Thea left, she would have seen no one.

Perhaps Daniel had come back to the compartment. She might have let him in, and they could have talked, but Thea highly doubted that Molly could have killed him. She had cried once when the village boys in Astermore had thrown punches at each other. The maid was so sweet and gentle that she would never harm a living creature, let alone another human being. It was inconceivable. And with how the girl reacted, she hadn't even known that Daniel was dead.

Molly dabbed her eyes with the handkerchief. "I can't believe it. I was just—"

"It's been very traumatizing," Thea said carefully, resting her hand on her maid's back.

Inside, she was dying to learn just how Molly knew Daniel. Watching the two of them had felt like she had been watching her own personal performance of Romeo and Juliet, starring Daniel and Molly.

This was sure to cause a scandal, one that would be hard to escape. It would cause an even bigger one if her maid was convicted of the murder. It would be even worse if it came out that Molly had been involved with the man before his death. Thea hoped for Molly's sake it would all blow over soon.

It was the kind of thing Thea didn't want to be caught up in, but she definitely didn't want her maid caught up in this mess under any circumstances. Molly was too sweet. The maid certainly would never survive the press nor being in prison.

The newspapermen were brutal, and they would be vicious towards anyone who thought murdering a man on the *Flying Scotsman* was a good idea. Thea shuddered to think what would happen if a reporter managed to get a photograph of Molly covered in Daniel's blood. Whatever shred of maternal instinct Thea had told her to protect Molly from the terrible fate that would befall her if she was tried in court and found guilty. She knew without a doubt that Molly was innocent, but Thea was also realistic enough to know that they would find her guilty despite the lack of evidence against her.

CHAPTER FIVE

IT WAS A WHILE BEFORE THE YORK POLICE ARRIVED AT THE train. The train had come into the station only moments after Inspector Thayne guided Thea and Molly out of the car. Like all the other first-class passengers, they had been confined to the parlor, lounge, and observation cars and were going a bit stir crazy.

"I swear, there is something wrong with you. I've never seen a girl so stupid—"

"Mother, please," the girl at the table across the aisle cried. "Stop," she begged.

Thea watched the mother and daughter from the platform. Up close, the girl was quite pretty. Thea had thought as much when she saw the girl before they boarded the train, but now her looks were ruined by red eyes. The mother was clearly frustrated with the idea of her daughter being so lovely. The suit the girl wore was a few seasons old, while the cut of the mother's suit was the latest couture. Since they were in first-class, Thea assumed they didn't lack means. It just seemed like the mother didn't wish to spend it on her daughter.

That was strange. Usually women who had daughters of a

marriageable age put all their money into paying for their daughters' wardrobe. They wanted them to look desirable so that the girls would marry well. To marry someone with money, one must pretend they had money, even if that was not the case.

Before her presentation and first Season, Thea's mother had brought her to Paris to have the latest fashions made and shipped back to England for her. The girl across the aisle had probably been presented or was going to be presented in the coming year, so the fact that she didn't have a new wardrobe was an enigma.

They were having a hushed argument, or more precisely, the mother was having an argument while the daughter appeared to plead with her.

"Mother, you can't keep doing this. It isn't right."

"It's not for you to decide," the mother snapped.

The girl lowered her voice, too low for Thea to make out what was being said without leaning closer. She truly admired the girl. She would have lost her composure with the woman by now and the argument would have escalated. She had inherited her mother's quick temper.

"Stop your sniveling," the woman sneered at her daughter.

Thea frowned, never more relieved to have such a supportive mother. If she had been this woman's daughter, she would have problems speaking, let alone being around people. She was impressed that the girl had even gotten a word in edgewise and didn't behave like a whimpering child. The reddened eyes could indicate crying, but they would also be from frustration, from being so angry with no possible way to express such emotions clearly.

It seemed Thea had been watching for longer than what was socially acceptable. The woman turned to her, glaring straight at her.

"Put your eyes back in your head and mind your own business, girl," the mother snapped at Thea. "This has nothing to do with you."

Thea bit her tongue to keep from saying something in return. To cause a scene so soon after the one in her compartment would not be in her or Molly's favor. Instead, she turned her head away and held to the hope that the police would arrive soon and put an end to this.

It took over an hour after discovering Daniel's body for the police to finally arrive at the station in York. If it had been an attempted murder and not a real one, it was sure to have become a real murder with their response time. It was truly shameful, especially after Inspector Thayne had arrived so promptly when she had screamed. The York police were not impressing her much.

The oddly assorted group that had arrived was not what she was expecting a group of policemen to look like. It was true that she didn't expect them all to look like Inspector Thayne, because few men did, but she certainly didn't expect such a ragtag group of individuals to be classified as police officers.

Unfortunately, she got the feeling that they were not far from the typical coppers that roamed the rest of London while the ones like Inspector Thayne actually solved the murders. Despite not knowing the men, she didn't like the idea that the policemen sent to solve Daniel's murder were so ragged a bunch. None of them looked very enthusiastic. Even fewer of them looked like they had experience. She got the impression that she was more qualified to investigate, though all she knew of detective work came from reading mystery novels. A handful of them looked like they had only just left primary school.

Nose all but pressed to the window of the car, she watched the platform like it was the stage of the most fascinating of plays and the policemen who had showed up were there for her entertainment. And perhaps it was. It had all the makings of one of those tragic theater performances her mother dragged her to, a hidden romance, a murder, a murderer on the loose, and a funny little cast of people aboard the train to amuse her while she waited.

Inspector Thayne joined them and shook their hands. With the lack of enthusiasm that they showed greeting him, Thea wondered what kind of effort they would put into the investigation. Would they go for the most obvious suspect? She glanced back to the interior of the train to where Molly was sitting at the table across from her.

Molly had stopped crying and her face was now dry. The girl was very pale and rigid, as if she knew that the moment she let her composure drop, she wouldn't be able to recover. The inspector had wrapped one of the Great Northern Railway's blankets around her to hide her bloodstained blouse. Molly had shrugged the blanket from her shoulders so that it no longer covered her shirt.

Inspector Thayne had offered to get Molly a change of clothes or to escort her to the washroom, but she had refused both. Molly looked like a woman who had just discovered her beloved was dead and wanted the world to know that he had been killed. She wanted to flaunt what had happened in their faces when so many of them were quick to turn a blind eye.

Seeing that display seemed to upset the other passengers. It felt like everyone on the train thought that Molly was too caught up in her grief to know what she was doing, but Thea knew that wasn't the case. After years of being by Thea's side, the girl understood perfectly what she was doing, but she didn't care.

Thea wasn't sure why, but she felt incredibly proud of her.

Thea swallowed as she watched her maid.

There was more to Molly and Daniel's relationship than

she had initially thought. Perhaps they truly had been Romeo and Juliet, secretly married and unable to be together because of their families. She remembered that Molly had mentioned once that she didn't get along with her parents.

An older, severe-looking man dressed in a suit, whom Thea assumed to be the detective in charge of the investigation, directed the officers on the platform. If she was going to guess, she'd say he was younger than Colonel Bantry but not by much. His hair was grayer than the Colonel's and his weathered skin spoke volumes about the kind of life he had lived. From the accusing look in his eyes, he already believed every single person on this train was guilty and was ready to convict them all at a moment's notice. Thea doubted he would be sympathetic to Molly's cause.

Following him was a considerably younger man in a constable's uniform. He looked more enthusiastic but seemed like he was too wide-eyed to be working a homicide, like this was his first case. While it was likely that it was his first murder, Thea wondered if it was his first investigation ever.

The older policeman approached the conductor. His constable scampered after him like an eager puppy tripping over his feet to keep up with him. When the older man stopped short, the constable had to stumble to keep from running into him.

Thea pressed her lips together to keep from giggling, despite the inappropriateness of the behavior. It wasn't as if they could hear her. It was only the fear of appearing insane before the police came to question her in respects to such a gruesome crime that stopped her. Surely her unfitting reactions alone would spell her as the murderess.

The police had a small entourage with them. Of the group, the most notable one was a man with a camera who looked as if he had just stepped out of an advertisement for Eastman Kodak. She imagined he was there to photograph the crime scene with the newest of technology. She cringed a little at the idea of a bunch of strange men roaming her compartment with her personal belongings, but there was nothing that could be done about it. Thea winced at how callous her thought was.

The coppers boarded the train, heading in the direction of the compartments. Thea shifted in her seat, restless and unable to relax as she waited for the inevitable to come. Any minute, the inspector and the rest of his retinue would come into the parlor car. She knew that as soon as they came, she would be forced to recount everything in excruciating detail. She would have to be extremely careful not to implicate Molly or herself.

Thea wished the police would come and ask their questions already, rather than study the scene. They were going to interrogate her and Molly and there was nothing either of them could do about it, so she wanted to get it over with. She was just getting anxious waiting and the more nervous she was, the guiltier she would look. Perhaps the policemen wanted her on edge so she would slip and incriminate herself, despite having not done anything wrong.

Finally, the police entered the parlor car and put Thea out of her misery.

"I'm Detective Chief Inspector Louis Stanton of the Leeds City Police." He motioned to the younger, uniformed man. It appeared that most of the other policemen had stayed behind in her compartment. "This is Constable Patrick Cooke. We're here about the death on the train. We ask that everyone stay on board and that no one leaves," the man spoke loudly, over the burst of whispers and mumbling that went up at his statement. "I want to speak with any witnesses. I want the person who found the body first."

Thea inhaled sharply.

The conductor nodded, motioning to her at her table. "This is Lady Theodora Prescott-Pryce. She's the one who found the body in her compartment."

Thea glanced at Inspector Thayne, who stood beside the inspector and the constable, then to Molly, who hadn't even appeared to hear what the inspector had said. She stared at Inspector Thayne until she caught his eye and he nodded. Thea wasn't entirely sure when she had begun to trust his opinion or him. Maybe it had to do with him seeing Molly covered in blood and not drawing the immediate and obvious conclusion that the maid was guilty.

Taking a deep breath and releasing it, Thea stood up and moved around the table. She walked the length of the car until she was within arm's length of DCI Stanton. Only then did she stop, eyeing him, trying to figure out exactly who the man she was dealing with was. The inspector appeared to be doing the same thing to her.

"Right," DCI Stanton said as he finished scrutinizing her, more for the benefit of the others beside him, as he turned back to the conductor, "Do you have somewhere where we can conduct the interviews?"

The conductor nodded and motioned back towards the corridor from which they had come. "Right this way, Inspector."

They filed out of the car, first the conductor, then the inspector and her, followed by the constable. Inspector Thayne stayed behind in the parlor car, taking a seat at the table with Molly. Thea nodded to herself, satisfied. She knew the inspector would take care of her maid.

"Are you alright, miss, I mean, your Ladyship, I mean, what do I mean?" the constable asked.

"My lady," she offered up. The constable blushed.

"Right. Er—are you alright, my lady?" he tried again, clearly flustered. From the way he spoke to her, she had trouble believing that he had ever met a woman that he wasn't related to before, let alone one with a title. She would be surprised if he had.

Thea gave him a smile, shakier than expected. Her hands were trembling, and she clenched them into fists, holding them against her stomach to try to control them so that the others wouldn't see. She didn't want DCI Stanton to see her so weak.

"I'm alright, Constable," she said, trying her best to sound positive, but not too positive. After all, she had found a dead body and she was just a poor, fragile lady. It wouldn't do to sound as if she actually had her wits about her. "It's just horrible about that poor man."

"It is, miss, er—my lady."

Normally, Thea would have laughed. She kept thinking she was fine, that it had hardly affected her, but her shaking hands and lack of nonchalance proved otherwise. She supposed that the reality was only just beginning to sink in. Perhaps that was why she was feeling so ill.

"Did you know him?" he asked softly.

"I had never met him before in my life."

The inspector turned to glare at them as they walked behind him. "What are you two whispering about?"

"Er- nothing, sir," the constable pipped up, "I was just asking Lady Theodora if she knew the deceased."

"Then it isn't nothing, Constable," the older man sneered. He reminded her an awful lot of the woman in the parlor with her daughter. Thea decided she didn't like him very much at all but liked the constable a great deal more. If anything, the younger man was much more polite than the inspector. "If you would leave the questions to me, it would be greatly appreciated."

"Sorry, sir," the constable said sheepishly, ducking his head in embarrassment. Thea tried to offer up an encouraging smile, but she wasn't entirely sure it didn't look like a grimace.

Glancing back, Thea noticed that the constable wasn't flushed in the usual telltale signs of chagrin, but instead seemed to be fighting a smirk. At this, Thea did smile and had to bite her cheek to keep it off her face. Despite how he had first presented himself, the young constable showed a great deal of promise compared to DCI Stanton.

Her hands were still trembling, despite the constable's attempts to put her at ease. She squeezed her fists tighter until her knuckles turned white.

The four of them passed through the sleeper cars and passed by the crime scene that had been her compartment. They kept walking, passing through the grueling masses of coach.

The cramped mix of passengers in coach shocked her more than it should have.

The filthy, unwashed sat in their tattered rags. They wore them proudly as if they were their Sunday best. There were those who could have passed into the first-class cars unnoticed, though their demeanor and hostile faces separated them from those Thea had left behind.

Children shrieked, their sharp screams piercing the air. The weary mothers and disgruntled fathers seemed to be down to their last nerve trying to silence them.

Just when Thea was sure that the train would go on forever, the four of them reached a small office-like space.

"If you will sit," DCI Stanton said rudely, motioning to the chair in front of the table. Thea sat down in it. "Stay here. I'll be back. Constable, stay with her." He turned back to the conductor. "Show me back to the crime scene."

The conductor nodded and showed him out. The door slammed shut behind them.

CHAPTER SIX

THE ROOM SEEMED TO BE SHRINKING IN ON ITSELF. THE AIR was so thick it was hard to breathe. The only window was dirty from the inside and so the whole office lacked light. The office didn't seem like it was well cared for. It was about the size of her compartment, maybe a little bigger, but it lacked the openness that her compartment had.

Thea swallowed hard as she played nervously with her hands. She glanced around the room, trying to find someplace for her eyes to settle as she waited for the inspector to come back.

"I'm sorry for making him yell at you, my lady," the constable said quietly from where he had been waiting by the door. "He's not usually so—"

Constable Cooke didn't finish his sentence, but somehow, he didn't need to. She doubted that whatever he would have said would have been true. The inspector seemed like a prickly sort of man who was always that way. She found it hard to believe that he was different the rest of the time.

Thea tried again to smile at the constable and failed miserably. He offered a small, comforting smile in return, moving to sit down across from her, but stopped just before he did.

"Can I get you anything while we wait, my lady? Some tea or something to eat?"

It seemed her initial impression of him was farther off than she had originally thought. Constable Cooke was not the bumbling, unsophisticated fool he had appeared to be in front of the inspector. He had quite good manners, far better than the inspector's and seemed quite used to dealing with women now. Surely such a short walk wouldn't make such a difference.

Thea shook her head, feeling like she had to catch her breath before speaking. "No thank you, Constable. I doubt I could stomach anything."

Her gut twisted. The horrors of the day were finally catching up with her. It didn't feel like the situation had fully sunk in.

"Completely understandable."

The young constable looked a little green too which made her feel a bit better. He had come after the body had been there, when it had been just a body. She had seen Daniel when he was alive and vibrant. She wasn't sure why, but that word seemed to fit the man despite not truly knowing him.

"Have you had many murders here?" she asked, trying desperately for the small talk she so despised. Anything to keep her mind off of her situation.

He shook his head. "I've only just joined the force here this year. I wouldn't know." He gave her a watery smile. "You're very brave, my lady. I don't think I could have been in your place and have been nearly as calm as you've been."

"I don't think it's hit me yet." Thea breathed in, deeply, trying to push down the panicked feeling bubbling in her chest. Any grim fascination she had had upon seeing the body had vanished. "It was just so horrible. There was a lot of blood." She shuddered. "Whoever killed him must have really hated him. When I saw him in the corridor before lunch, he was very polite. It seemed like such a terrible way to die."

The constable's shoulders drooped. He pulled the chair out and sat down finally, folding his hands in front of him on the table. He looked defeated, like as if seeing such a young man dead forced him to deal with his own mortality. Perhaps it did.

"It is," he agreed. Then, as if realizing her words, he spoke again, "You met him then?"

She shook her head, biting her lip. She didn't mean to give the impression that she had truly known the man. "Only for a brief second in the hall. I was heading into the restaurant car as he was coming out of it. He moved to the side so I could pass."

The constable smiled slightly, but there was some sadness behind it. "Yes, I see what you mean then. It does seem like he was very polite."

They sat in silence for a long moment, until the inspector came back into the room, door slamming open against the wall. Constable Cooke scrambled out of his chair, eyes wide, his frightened but loyal puppy act back firmly in place as he moved quickly towards the wall.

———

DCI Stanton had returned to the office alone, his face the very image of fury. Thea's heart stuttered as she wondered if he might strike her. She had heard once that that wasn't an entirely uncommon behavior by policemen. At the same time, Thea wondered if Constable Cooke would let him.

"You were the one who found the body?" Inspector Stanton prompted, with no formalities or pleasantries. She didn't answer, overcome momentarily by panic bubbling in her throat.

Thea winced as the older man smacked his hand on the

table, bringing her back into the moment. He towered over her in a way that forced her to either lean back against her corset or strain her neck uncomfortably. Neither presented an option that allowed her to breathe. "Yes, sir, I did."

"And he was in your compartment?"

"Yes, he—"

"You had let him in your compartment?" he fired off, before she could even answer, more leading than questioning.

Her blood boiled. Stanton was accusing her of killing him. She knew he would. She breathed out, then in, deeply, until she had calmed down enough to speak. Fed up, she crossed her arms defensively, leveling her head and giving the best impersonation she could have of her grandmother.

"Inspector, I didn't even know the man. I only saw him once in the corridor between the sleeper and restaurant cars. I didn't even say a word to him. He only excused himself when he moved out of my way in the hall. I have no idea why he was found in my compartment."

"So what you're saying is that you didn't know him?"

Thea nearly screamed in frustration. It was like the man was purposely trying her patience, like he thought that if he played dumb, she would admit to killing Daniel. If the inspector kept at it though, Thea was sure she would kill someone on this train and that someone was standing directly across from her.

"That's exactly what I'm saying, Inspector."

"But your maid knew him? She was the one who let him into your compartment?"

Thea bit her tongue. She considered lying, but that would be pointless and would only make her look guilty. Any witness could easily verify that Molly had known the man and had screamed his name when they found him. Molly had been a wreck and so many had seen it. All it took was one look at her covered in Daniel's blood to draw the wrong conclusions.

"I don't know. I wasn't with her. I was in the restaurant car." Thea stared across the table at him.

"So your maid never came into the restaurant car?"

Thea shook her head. "She was eating a sandwich from the trolley when I left to go to lunch."

Inspector Stanton pursed his lips and nodded. He reached into his jacket, pulling something from his pocket, wrapped in a paper bag. He turned the bag upside down, the contents spilling onto the table between them.

"Do you recognize this?" Stanton demanded from her.

Thea stared down at the shiny object. She leaned closer and realized it was a red-colored gem and gold hair pin coated in blood. It had to have been the one that Daniel had been holding, the one he had wielded as a weapon against his killer. Thea could see now that it was gaudy, not to her tastes in the least. She was sure she had seen a set that looked like it before but couldn't place where she had seen it.

Up close, she could see the scratches on the gold and how the stone had been reset in it. Whatever the jewel had been before must have been worth more than the metal. Perhaps it had been pulled from the pin and sold for money.

"It's a hatpin," Thea said as dryly as she could manage. If Inspector Stanton could pretend he was stupid, then two could play at that game.

Stanton crossed his arms, glaring down at her. Thea glared back until she sighed and relented.

"That was what he was holding, wasn't it? The man in my compartment. Daniel," she corrected herself. "I saw something shiny in his hand when Molly came in."

"Have you ever seen this before?"

She took another good long look at it, then shook her head. "It's not one of mine. Garnet wouldn't match any of my hats."

"Perhaps it belongs to your maid."

Thea stared down at the pin. It had clearly belonged to a

woman of means, someone who would have always had the latest and most fashionable clothes and accessories. Of course, fashionable was a relative term.

Molly was by no means wealthy. Any money the girl made, she saved. She had been saving her pay since the day she had started working for Thea's family. But years of Molly dressing her told Thea that the girl had much better taste than that.

"That's unlikely." She glanced at it, "See the metal? It's real gold, but the gems are fake. They look like they were pried out when they were replaced. The woman who bought this pin came from money. She was probably concerned about it but also wanted to keep up appearances. That's not Molly."

Not on her salary, Thea would have liked to say, but she could imagine how everyone involved would have cringed. She knew better than to discuss money with anyone outside of the family.

A puzzled expression came over Stanton's face, almost as if he was mocking her. He knew something she didn't, and she didn't like it.

"Are you so sure about that, my lady?" She frowned, not liking where this was going. He pulled out his notepad, reading it off to her. "Miss Margaret Forbes is the daughter of Ambrose Forbes, of the London law firm Pembroke and Forbes. The folks down at Scotland Yard assured me they live quite comfortably. Therefore she would have easily been able to afford that hatpin."

Thea frowned harder, staring at the pin as if it held the answers she was looking for. She had never been so wrong about anyone before. Molly couldn't possibly be rich.

"But that's impossible. Molly doesn't come from money. She couldn't possibly have! Why on earth would she work as a maid if she did?"

"Perhaps to hide from her former husband, Mr. Talbot.

Then he tracked her down and threatened to reveal her secret. And that was why she killed him."

Thea sputtered out a laugh with more bravado than she actually felt. It sounded so completely absurd.

"Husband?" she asked. "Molly's barely twenty."

Molly had come to work for Thea's family when Molly had been fifteen. She had been very private about her life before. Thea had asked, but the girl had always been rather vague, so Thea had just assumed that Molly had been an orphan. Was the real reason she had never said anything was that Molly had been married the entire time she had worked for Thea's family?

But this man said that Molly was rich, or at least her family was. It made no sense that she would come to work as a maid if her family had money. And how did Daniel know how to find her if she had been hiding from him? Why wouldn't her wealthy family protect her from such a man?

Also, Thea found the idea that Molly had been hiding from Daniel, who she assumed was Mr. Talbot, ridiculous. She definitely wouldn't have kissed him the way she had, too full of passion to be given by someone who was terrified by the other. Even if Molly had been lying for all these years, Thea didn't believe that anyone was that good of an actress.

There was much more to the story than Stanton knew. Of that, Thea was certain.

"That is the most ridiculous thing I have ever heard," she continued on with more bravado than she actually felt.

The older man scoffed. "It's hardly ridiculous, my lady." He eyed her critically. "Just how well did you know your maid?"

"Well enough to know she didn't kill anyone." She crossed her arms, feeling a little like a petulant child. She stared down the older man, giving him the same look her grandmother liked to give her when Thea had done something the older woman didn't approve of. Thea knew deep down that even if Molly had lied about who she was, she didn't have a mean bone in her body. She was not a murderess.

Inspector Stanton sighed heavily, clearly exasperated with her.

"You may go," he told her. "Constable, show Lady Theodora out and bring in Miss Forbes."

Constable Cooke hopped to. "Yes, sir."

Thea rose from the chair, sticking her nose up as if trying to tell the inspector she thought he was beneath her. It was all a show, of course. She was still shaking incessantly, but she clenched her fists tightly so that the inspector wouldn't see her hands quivering as she left the room.

THEA WALKED BEHIND CONSTABLE COOKE AS THEY MADE THEIR way back towards the parlor car. She watched him. The constable was walking much more confidently now that Inspector Stanton wasn't around to observe him.

"I'm sorry about him, my lady. He can be a bit much when he gets his mind set on an idea."

Thea smiled, despite the fact that he couldn't see it.

"That's quite alright, Constable. I know he was only trying to do his job." She sighed, drawn out and overly dramatic. "I do hope you find the killer soon. This whole business is just dreadful."

Constable Cooke, thankfully, didn't see through her act. The last thing she wanted was for the police to think she was being insincere.

"Well, here we are, my lady," the constable said, moving to the side as she entered the car.

Thea turned and gave him her best nervous smile. "Thank you, Constable."

She moved back towards her previously abandoned chair, Constable Cooke following behind her. Inspector Thayne had ordered tea for him and Molly. Miracle of all miracles, it appeared he had managed to get Molly to drink a little of it.

The maid was still rather out of it. Her arms were wrapped tightly around her body, hugging her stomach. Molly had finally washed her hands. The poor thing was still so upset. She was as white as a sheet. Thea was honestly surprised that Molly hadn't fainted.

Inspector Thayne watched her as she approached them. He seemed satisfied that she was okay, but he didn't say anything as she sat down.

Constable Cooke inclined his head to her. "Please let me know if you think of anything else, my lady."

"Of course, Constable." Thea smiled. She had no intention of letting Constable Cooke know anything. He was kind and gentle, though something about him rang insincere. She wouldn't tell him anything unless Molly's life depended on it.

CHAPTER SEVEN

Thea relaxed into the chair as she watched Constable Cooke leave. She turned her wrist to look at her watch.

"You were gone nearly an hour," Inspector Thayne said as he looked at his pocket watch. Thea was more surprised than she should have been to see how simple of a watch it was. "Would you like some tea?"

Thea shrugged, staring at the time mocking her from her wrist. That couldn't possibly be right, but the watch confirmed that she had been with DCI Stanton and Constable Cooke for an hour.

Had Inspector Stanton thought she was guilty? Had he thought that by leaving her in there to stew that it would somehow make her confess to a crime she hadn't committed? Perhaps he had been trying to make her slip up, to make it sound like Molly was guilty.

"The whole affair is a ridiculous farce," Thea declared. "Inspector Stanton has already decided who he thinks is guilty. Nothing he discovers is going to make a lick of difference."

"I agree," Inspector Thayne said, much to Thea's surprise.

She blinked, looking up at him. She had never actually expected him to hold the same opinion that she did.

A steward brought Thea a cup and saucer and poured some tea for her before he cleared Molly's cup. Thea left it on the table. She wasn't thirsty, couldn't possibly drink now. The liquid was dark and steaming. It smelt delicious and made her stomach twist.

Inspector Thayne was faring much better than Molly or her. He downed his cup and poured another for himself.

"You should really drink that," he told her.

She shook her head. "I couldn't possibly."

"Put a few sugar cubes in it. It'll help." Thea couldn't help but grimace. Her heart still felt like it was racing. Sugar was the last thing she needed. Not only that, she hated sugar in her tea.

"I think I'm alright for now."

Inspector Thayne had a mind of his own. He reached across to the sugar pot and dropped three or four cubes into her tea.

"Drink."

She didn't feel like arguing, so she drank the overly sweetened liquid. It caught in her throat, burning and stinging. Thea coughed and tried to cover her mouth with her handkerchief.

The inspector flagged over a passing steward. "Can you bring her a glass of water, please?"

"Of course, sir," the man said, bobbing his head.

"I don't need—" she started to protest, her coughs subsiding. The steward returned near-instantly with the glass, placing it on the table before her. She sighed. "Thank you," she said but glared at Inspector Thayne. He seemed unfazed.

"You need to drink and stay hydrated."

Thea bit her tongue. Who did he think he was telling her what to do? Her father? Her brother? He certainly wasn't her husband as if she'd ever want to marry the likes of someone like him.

Seeing as he wasn't relenting and she didn't feel like fighting him on it, Thea picked up the glass to drink. The water was barely able to stay in the glass, sloshing wildly against the sides. She didn't need to look up at the man across from her to know he was giving her a knowing look.

Thea glanced up through her lashes to check and sure enough, Inspector Thayne was doing just that. When had she gotten to know him so well? She had only just met him and had only one real conversation with him.

Not wanting to hear the inspector tell her again, Thea brought the glass to her lips and drank before it could splash onto her. Inspector Thayne had a sly smirk on his face. She was tempted to dip her fingers into the water and splash them at him.

***

Constable Cooke stepped back into the car, looking around nervously. Thea had to hand it to him. He pulled off the whole incompetence act rather well. The constable looked back and forth between her and Inspector Thayne, moving towards their table.

"Sir," he started to say, then saw her. "Sorry, my lady." He turned back to Inspector Thayne. "Sir, DCI Stanton asked me to come get you."

Inspector Thayne drank the last of his tea and stood up.

"If you will excuse me, Lady Thea, Miss Forbes," the inspector said softly, bowing slightly to each of them in his usual charming fashion.

"Excuse me," a matronly woman called, standing up from the table behind Thea to move into the path of the two men as they tried to leave. "Constable, have you looked into what I told you about?"

"I'm sorry, ma'am. I haven't yet. If you will excuse us."

Constable Cooke tried to dart around the woman, but she was having none of it.

"Constable, you promised you would find the person who took my pearls."

"Mrs. Beauvale, I will see that it gets looked into," the officer said, his face flushed. He moved around her and the woman let out a huff of annoyance as Inspector Thayne followed the constable out of the car.

"Excuse me," Thea said to the woman as she moved to reclaim her seat. "Did you say your pearls were missing?"

Mrs. Beauvale sniffled dramatically. "Yes, right out of my compartment. You're missing something as well?"

Thea shook her head. "No." But then she thought about it. She hadn't actually looked in her compartment to see if she was missing anything. Mr. Talbot could have interrupted the thief in the act. Only last week she had heard about a man stabbed in his own home when he tried to stop a robber. "At least, I don't think so."

The older woman patted her hand comfortingly.

"You wouldn't be the first. Mr. Worsley, that poor, dear man, had his pocket watch picked right off of him not long after he boarded. It's criminal the way they'll just let anyone onto these trains."

Thea nodded and gave what she hoped was a smile. Mrs. Beauvale quickly lost interest in her and turned back to the others at her table. Thea turned around in her seat, letting out a sigh of relief.

Molly was in no state to be company right now, so she was back to her boredom again, it seemed, and this time she didn't even have the policemen on the platform to entertain her.

Thea fidgeted in her seat. She hated being so exposed and out in the open. It was hard to be in public, in front of so many people, when she felt like she could barely hold herself together. The compartments were off-limits for the moment, and she had no idea of when they'd be allowed to return to those carriages. She wouldn't be able to relax until she was away from their judgmental eyes.

It had been mere minutes after Constable Cooke had retrieved Inspector Thayne before he was back for Molly. The girl had risen from the table numbly. The constable gently guiding her towards the front of the train and out of the car, on to where Inspector Stanton was surely waiting for Molly to interrogate her in the same militaristic style he had Thea.

The ostentatious mother was back at it, screaming at her daughter in the same tone that she had been using before Thea had left to be questioned. The daughter's face had lost some of the redness it had earlier. The young woman also seemed to have given up on pleading with her mother. Not that Thea blamed her. She would have given up hours ago.

Thea didn't dare risk staring at them. She didn't want to get yelled at by the mother again.

Of course, that was when Mrs. Livingston floated through as she talked to a steward who seemed desperate to get away.

"I just want my book from my compartment. I'm not asking you to let me rob the Bank of England or something crazy like that," she drawled in that over-exaggerated accent of hers.

"Mrs. Livingston, I'm not at liberty to go through the compartments," the steward said the words as if he had said them a dozen times to her already. He was a young man, barely more than a child, and looked like he might faint under the woman's intense scrutiny. "Besides, the police won't allow anyone into the sleeper cars at the moment."

"They can't possibly expect us to stay packed like sardines in here with no entertainment, can they?" Mrs. Livingston tossed her head back, "Are you gonna sing for us, sonny?"

The poor steward sputtered, turning as red as could be. "I'm afraid the police don't care very much about what you do,

Mrs. Livingston, so long as it's not in the sleeper cars right now."

The American gave an overdramatic sigh, throwing her hand against her face like she might faint. Thea pressed her lips together to hide a smile. The woman was putting on a performance for them.

"That is a perfect example of what I don't want you to become," the mother whispered condescendingly to her daughter. "There's nothing more gauche than to show the entire world what you're feeling. She's no better than a common street whore flaunting herself like that."

The change was near-instantaneous. Mrs. Livingston whipped around on the woman. Her face turned stormy and her sunny disposition was a thing of the past. In her place was an angry goddess as she stalked forward towards the table, her prey in her sights.

Thea raised her brow in amusement. This was bound to be entertaining, for the moment at least.

"How dare you?" Mrs. Livingston thundered.

"How dare I?" the mother asked haughtily. "How dare you make such an utter spectacle of yourself in front of all of us. It is entirely one thing if you wish to do so, but to subject us all to it is vulgar."

"Mother," the daughter begged softly.

"Quiet, Nora. The adults are talking."

The girl, Nora, clenched her jaw. Thea thought she saw the girl ball her hands by her sides.

"And you called me uncivilized?" Mrs. Livingston asked cheekily. "At least I don't speak so demeaningly to everyone around me. No wonder why your daughter's so embarrassed by you." The mother hmphed and the American woman eyed her up and down. "What I find truly fascinating is that you call me uncivilized and yet we have the same taste in jewelry. I have a brooch just like that one."

The mother's face became like stone as she stood and beckoned for her daughter to follow.

"Come, Nora. I won't tolerate being in the same space with such garbage."

The girl opened her mouth to protest, only to see her mother halfway to the next car. Nora sighed, shoulders hunched as she stood and turned to Mrs. Livingston. "I apologize for my mother."

The American woman shook her head, giving her a small smile. "It's not your fault, darling."

The girl returned the smile shyly, running after her mother as quickly as the rules of proper society would allow.

"Good riddance," Mrs. Livingston muttered under her breath when both mother and daughter were out of earshot.

Amazingly, the rest of the occupants of the car were already back minding their business. That was very much like high society. A bunch of busybodies who all liked to pretend that they weren't.

Then, to Thea's great horror, the American woman spotted her sitting alone. Thea tried to duck her head, to go through the contents of her handbag, anything but meet the other woman's eyes. Still Mrs. Livingston didn't get the hint and sat down across from her.

"Can you believe the nerve of some people?" the American scoffed loudly in disbelief. "They think they're better than me."

Well, Thea thought, *Nora's mother was wrong on that account.* Both women were equally loud and obnoxious and worse yet, they were both apparently oblivious to that fact.

"What is with you English?" Mrs. Livingston asked, not maliciously, but in that straightforward way she had that seemed so out of place.

"Most of us don't like to make a scene," Thea said dryly. "There's a small handful that don't seem to realize when they do."

"God bless 'em," she said.

Thea sighed, looking away. She had this area all to herself before and now the American woman was going to talk her ear off. Mrs. Livingston had clearly never learned to take a hint before or didn't care to do so.

"Was there something that you wanted, Mrs. Livingston?" she asked formally.

The American shook her head. "No, I was just looking for something to do. These policemen won't even let me get a book to read from out of my compartment. It's unbelievable!"

"Ah."

"Do you mind?" Mrs. Livingston asked, motioning to the teapot and the cup on the table between them.

"By all means, help yourself," Thea said sarcastically as the woman reached across to do just that.

Mrs. Livingston smiled at her, clearly not recognizing her tone. Or perhaps the American did and just didn't care. Thea wouldn't put it past her.

But then again, maybe she didn't and just thought that Thea was being genuine. She grimaced, feeling a little bit guilty. After all, the woman had not been unpleasant to her. In fact, Mrs. Livingston had been more decent to her than those she had known for years. It was not her fault that the American woman acted in a manner better suited for a barn than polite society.

Deciding that she should make more of an effort to be friendly with the other woman, Thea waved down the steward to ask for some crackers or biscuits to go with the tea.

CHAPTER EIGHT

It was sometime later before Mrs. Livingston had gotten bored and left in search of a quiet spot in the observation car with a fascinating view of the station. Thea found herself at the opposite end of the car, trying to get comfortable in one of the larger chairs as she watched the other passengers strolling into the lounge and the observation car.

Thea was sure most were hanging around the bar. Since the train had not departed from the station and no one was allowed to leave, everyone was getting quite restless. The liquor did little to help their growing displeasure and so she avoided the lounge and dining cars.

Molly had yet to return from her interrogation with Inspector Stanton. Inspector Thayne hadn't reemerged from whatever hole the policemen had made him disappear into either.

The passengers remaining in the parlor liked to gossip loudly, most of them gathering around the cafe tables. Thea didn't know where any of them got their information from, but some of it seemed quite valid.

Thea had heard a few of the other passengers talking

about how they were going to disconnect the carriage her compartment was in from the rest of the train, so that the police in York could continue to examine it. She hoped that if this rumor was true that they would allow her to collect her belongings first.

Her month-long trip to Scotland to visit her cousins would turn into a lifetime without her books and embroidery. Among her belongings was a sampler that she had been working on for the last month and she wasn't going to let them confiscate that from her. Thea needed those things if she was to stay sane while in Scotland with her much more confident cousins.

It wasn't that her family was bad company. She just found the dinner parties, hunting parties, and other social affairs that would occur while she was there to be a total bore.

Her younger cousin Charlotte was a rather plain-looking girl, but she was always dressed gorgeously in the latest fashions. This would be the first year she would actually be participating in the Season in London. From what Thea had gathered from their letters, Charlie was beyond excited to go, but mostly for the new wardrobe that she would have to get for it. The girl loved clothing as much as she loved her own life and had been making plans for her court dress from the time she could hold a pen in her hand.

Her older cousin Anthony was perhaps the most handsome man alive and the most charming one too. Thea had yet to meet a woman who wasn't madly in love with Anthony. Even she had followed him around doe-eyed when they were younger, but she had realized the ridiculousness of her actions when she grew older.

Her legs felt stiff from being stuck in one place for so long. Her body felt like it was buzzing, like she was a child in a candy shop who had eaten far too much sugar.

Thea stood up from the chair. She needed to get out of there. She needed to move. She needed air.

With small, quick steps, Thea moved through the car, past the chairs and people all milling around. Some were talking, holding lengthy conversations with each other. Others were reading or had various projects, like knitting or embroidery or were writing letters.

A sharp stab of jealousy shot through her. It all was so easy for them to just go on as if nothing had happened. She couldn't stand to be in there another moment longer.

Thea made her way to the lavatory, slipping through the corridors as swiftly as she could. It was more spacious than she remembered from her past travels, perhaps because no one else was in there.

For a brief moment, the idea of hiding and staying there until the train began moving again seemed appealing. Logically she knew it wouldn't work. Someone would come in and discover her too quickly.

Thea turned on the water. The water was cool and refreshing. She scrubbed at her hands. Despite having gloves on when she found the body, she felt like her hands were still coated in blood. She knew it was all in her head.

Her reflection in the mirror was too pale, so she splashed a little water on her cheeks and used a towel to dry. It helped very little. She felt like all the blood had been drained from her body.

She swayed dangerously. Her hands shot out to grab the sides of the sink, just barely keeping herself upright. A wave of nausea washed over her, but she closed her eyes and fought against it. She swallowed hard. It started to pass, but the ringing in her ears remained.

Thea opened her eyes, feeling a bit more stable. The room was no longer spinning around her.

Taking a deep breath, she tried to compose herself before she could go back out there again. It wouldn't do to let anyone see her flinch.

Thea walked back into the parlor and sat down by the window. From her vantage point, she could see Molly being escorted off the train in handcuffs. Constable Cooke was trying to be gentle, kind, but DCI Stanton didn't seem to be having any of that. Inspector Thayne was following them, but he stopped when Inspector Stanton turned to him and said something. From what little Thea could see of Stanton's face, it did not appear to be too pleasant.

Thea gripped the edge of the chair, watching the platform. Molly kept glancing back, clearly worried and terrified. Thea couldn't help but wonder, ever so briefly, was Molly guilty?

She shook her head. That was impossible. Molly couldn't kill a fly, let alone another human being. Her maid had to be innocent which meant Inspector Stanton had made a mistake. Worse yet, the police didn't believe they made a mistake, because they were arresting her maid.

Thea vowed that she would find the person who had actually killed Daniel Talbot.

CHAPTER NINE

THE FOOD BEING SERVED SMELLED DELICIOUS, BUT THEA DIDN'T feel much like eating. She kept cutting the same piece of meat over and over, just going through the motions. Her stomach had twisted itself into knots and she didn't think she'd be able to eat a bite. How could the police arrest poor, sweet Molly?

A young man with sandy hair and an overly confident, but charming grin slipped into the chair across from her. There was something oddly familiar about him, but she couldn't put her finger on it. Thea hadn't felt much like company and had deliberately sat at a two-person table by herself, hoping to finish dinner before anyone else joined her. Obviously that hope was in vain.

"Lady Theodora," the man greeted. "James Poyntz of the West End Gazette. How do you do?"

He offered his hand across the table and Thea stared at it, a bit unnerved. His smile waned slightly, and he withdrew his hand.

"Right. I apologize for interrupting your dinner. If it wouldn't be too much of an imposition, would you mind if I ask you a few questions about the murder?"

Thea took a deep breath. She hated being in the spotlight like this. She had known it would only be a matter of time before some reporter jumped at the scandal.

She could already see the headline on tomorrow's paper reading "Murder on the *Flying Scotsman*."

"What is it you wanted to know?" she asked warily.

"I heard it was your compartment and that you were the one who found the body." Thea swallowed, dreading whatever would come out of his mouth next. Mr. Poyntz reached into his jacket pocket, retrieving a small notebook that he held up for her to see. "You don't mind if I take some notes, do you? I don't want to forget anything."

She smiled wryly and hoped it didn't look too much like a grimace. "By all means."

Mr. Poyntz nodded, uncapping his pen. He wrote down her name at the top of the page, then looked up at her.

"What was your reaction when you saw the body in your compartment?"

Thea fought herself from raising her eyebrows. Was he serious? Was that really the first question he wanted to ask her. What did he think her reaction would be to finding a strange man dead in her compartment?

"I was terrified," Thea lied, giving the answer she figured he wanted. But she hadn't been scared at the time. She had been confused; she still was confused. "It was very frightening. I had never seen something so horrible."

The last part, of course, wasn't a lie.

He nodded emphatically and jotted down some quick notes. He blinked and looked up.

"How does it feel to know you've been living with a cold-blooded murderess?"

Thea ground her teeth. She was so sick of hearing that today. If one more person told her Molly killed Mr. Talbot, she might snap and kill someone herself. "Molly Forbes did not kill anyone."

"Can I quote you on that?" Mr. Poyntz asked her, and Thea pressed her tongue between her teeth to keep from saying anything too sarcastic. Then she noticed that Mr. Poyntz was waiting for her response, so she forced herself to think for a moment before she answered.

"Yes, you can," she all but spat out. "And you can also put down that the police are working to find the real killer."

He jotted her words down in the book, pausing as he got to her second statement. The look he gave her was one a person would give to a small child, as if he couldn't believe she was being that naïve. "You really believe that? I mean you believe that the police are still looking to find whoever killed the man?"

She didn't. Thea was positive that they would give up, having arrested Molly. Justice wouldn't prevail, but she didn't want him to quote her in the paper as saying that.

He capped the pen and set it down. "Off the record, I don't think it adds up. Motive, means, and opportunity. Miss Forbes might have had those, but she doesn't remind me of any of the cold-blooded killers I've met."

"Have you met many?"

Mr. Poyntz lip quirked. "I've met my fair share on assignment. I was watching Miss Forbes when she was in the parlor early. She reacted more like a widow."

Thea paused. The secret kiss in her compartment. The tenderness shared between them. The way Molly had reacted upon seeing the body. If Molly was Mr. Talbot's wife, those actions made a lot more sense.

"Not only that. I saw the body. It looked like he fought back." Thea's head jerked up in shock. She thought she had been the only one to have seen that.

"Molly wasn't injured," she whispered.

Whoever had killed him might have been hurt. Thea

thought back to the blood on Mr. Talbot's hands, under his fingernails. Mr. Talbot would have had to scratch quite deeply to get that much blood on him. She could almost visualize him grabbing at the person, trying to get them to stop. His fingers would have had to dig into his killer's leg, through their clothing, in order to get that kind of blood. A man's trousers were too thick to draw blood through.

But then Thea remembered that there had been a woman's boot print on the floor outside her door. Maybe the blood had dripped down the killer's leg and that was why there had only been part of a print. What if the killer had been a woman, just not the woman that the police had arrested?

Thea stood up, offering her hand to the newspaperman. He took it.

"Thank you, Mr. Poyntz. You have been very informative."

With that, she turned and left. She had an inspector to find.

CHAPTER TEN

THEA WENT TO THE CONDUCTOR IN HER SEARCH FOR INSPECTOR Thayne. He reluctantly told her that the inspector was back on the train and that the compartments were once again accessible. Thea managed to coax the inspector's compartment number from the conductor.

With that information in hand, she marched on to the inspector's private compartment and knocked.

While she wasn't thrilled to discover that Mr. Thayne actually worked for Scotland Yard, right now it seemed like he was Molly's only hope. But he had been kind to Molly and to her, so Thea was hoping he believed in Molly's innocence, unlike his colleagues.

The door slid open, revealing Inspector Thayne.

"Lady Thea," he greeted.

"Inspector Thayne," she said coolly.

"I was just getting ready to come look for you." He sighed. "DCI Stanton believes you know something more about the murder than what you told him." He stepped to the side. "Won't you please come in?"

She entered and Inspector Thayne slid the door closed

behind her. She swallowed slightly. She had never been in such a small space alone with a man before.

Inspector Thayne sat down, but Thea remained standing. She felt far too restless to sit down again.

"I don't know what DCI Stanton thinks I know that I haven't already told him." Thea sighed, glancing out the window as another train pulled up to the adjoining platform. "I came back from lunch. I found Mr. Talbot's body in my compartment. I screamed. Molly came in. I don't know what else I can tell him or you."

Inspector Thayne shook his head. "I need you to tell me step by step what happened, starting from the moment you left the restaurant car."

Thea let out a cry of frustration. "This is ridiculous. I've told you everything already. Molly didn't do anything!"

"DCI Stanton charged Miss Forbes for murder and since the murder took place in your compartment, he tried to say that you knew about it ahead of time and were an accomplice, but there's no proof so he had to drop the case he was trying to make against you."

Thea grasped at the wall. The air was all being sucked out of the compartment. It was making her head spin. It felt like someone had reached into her chest and was holding her lungs so that she couldn't inhale properly.

She had nothing to do with Mr. Talbot's murder. She hadn't even known the man. What possible reason would she have had to help kill him?

Thea clawed at the window, trying to get it open to get more air, but her fingers just couldn't gain purchase on the sill.

Never in her wildest dreams did Thea ever think that Stanton would accuse her of helping to murder a man she had never even met.

The floor had gone out from under her feet.

"Thea," Inspector Thayne muttered, but she didn't hear

him, "Theodora, you need to sit down," he commanded softly. Her ears were ringing, and she was swaying dangerously. His hands were all that were holding her up. He guided her down onto the bench and she crumbled.

Inspector Thayne reached for an object on the rack above her head and she flinched despite knowing that she had no reason to. He pulled down a coat.

"You've been through a great ordeal," Inspector Thayne spoke softly, wrapping his coat around her, running his hands up and down her arms as he did to warm her. Thea hadn't realized how cold she felt until he had bundled her into the jacket. He didn't seem to realize what he was doing until he pulled his hands back quickly.

"You don't think I helped killed him, do you?" she asked suddenly as he began to leave.

He shook his head. "No. He was dead before you got there. Besides, you were with me at lunch at the time of the murder. I'm afraid that doesn't rule out your maid. She even admitted to not having an alibi, to having been with him just before his death. She also admitted to being married to him briefly, but it was voidable as they lacked the proper parental consent and she had used the name Molly Anne Forbes on her banns instead of Margaret Susan Forbes, so her parents hadn't picked up on it."

Thea fought down a gasp. Her suspicions were confirmed then.

"She might have been married to him once, but Molly would never have killed him," Thea declared.

If there was one thing in which Thea was certain, it was that Molly had loved Mr. Talbot. Molly was so prim and proper that Thea highly doubted Molly would have let someone she had been married to however many years ago kiss her and call her by her Christian name if she didn't. But perhaps that gave her motive in DCI Stanton's book.

Inspector Thayne gave her a sad smile, one that felt surprisingly not condescending to her. Just because she was sure Molly didn't do it didn't make her naïve. It certainly didn't make her stupid and she was glad that Inspector Thayne knew that.

"Do you think there's any way I'll be able to see her?" Thea asked him.

The inspector looked down, but then glanced back to her. "I'll see what I can arrange with DCI Stanton. In the meantime, the train won't be going anywhere. You can stay in here, if you'd like."

Thea nodded, his words not really registering in her mind before he disappeared from the compartment. Her whole body ached. Her lungs still felt like they were burning, like they were too heavy for her body. Her throat almost felt swollen.

Worst of all, Thea felt very deeply tired and she fought back several yawns. She could have easily curled up on the bench and fallen asleep. Inspector Thayne's coat was very warm, and she was cold and emotionally drained. It would have been so easy to just move to the side and rest her head on the wall and let her eyelids droop.

Inspector Thayne's return jerked her awake from her near-sleep state. She jumped as the door slid open.

"I brought you some tea."

He passed her a steaming cup and Thea took it numbly, sipping at it. The china rattled in her hands. She blushed and separated the saucer and the cup to stop the noise. She didn't think her hands would ever stop trembling again.

Thea wrinkled her nose at the sweetness of the tea, resisting the urge to spit it back into the cup. She only just barely managed. It had far more sugar than she ever drank. She gagged as she swallowed it.

"You need to drink the whole thing. It'll help," Inspector Thayne said softly as he moved to open the window.

"Why do you keep adding sugar in my tea?" she asked him.

"It helps with the shaking," he said knowingly, looking pointedly at her hands.

Thea hated to admit it, but the sickly tea was helping. The room had almost stopped spinning and the fresh air made her feel like she could actually catch her breath. She breathed in, forcing herself to hold it before releasing it.

Inspector Thayne sat down across from her, their knees almost touching. She shivered.

"I know this is hard to hear, but you have to consider all the possibilities."

Thea set the empty cup aside on the bench. It rattled a little in its saucer.

"Hard to hear? You're telling me dear little Molly Forbes killed someone! It's impossible!" she exclaimed.

Thea wasn't convinced that the same girl who read Sherlock Holmes would be so careless as to murder a man in her compartment with no alibi whatsoever. Molly would never hurt anyone.

But Thea wasn't going to tell Inspector Thayne that. She realized that could make them both look even more guilty.

Thea stood, unable to sit so close to him any longer, not when he was sitting there so calmly, so collected. Her body felt like it was buzzing again, like she had too much energy.

She paced inside the compartment. Keeping the coat wrapped firmly around her, she moved over to the window. It was dark outside. The electric lights on the platform cast unnatural shadows.

Her watch said it had only been a little over two hours since Molly's arrest. It felt so much longer.

"We have to find who did this and clear Molly's name," she declared.

"We?" Inspector Thayne asked amused, crossing his arms as he leaned against the back of the bench.

Thea turned to stare at him. She couldn't get a real handle on him. He was a detective, but did he actually believe that Molly was innocent? Would he help her even if he thought she was?

"I am going to find out who did this and clear Molly's name," she corrected, "and I don't care if you help me or not."

He chuckled.

"Don't get all worked up, Lady Thea," he teased, "I never said I wasn't going to help you." His smile faded as he turned more serious, "I wouldn't like to see that young woman hanged for murder any more than you would."

"They'll have to let her go if we find the real killer, right?"

He nodded. "Then that's what we have to do."

"We'll find them. You have my word on that."

Inspector Thayne stood, moving over to her to take her hands in his, holding them tightly. They were much warmer than hers. Hers felt so cold. Inspector Thayne must have felt that, because he rubbed them between his like he was trying to warm them up.

Thea looked up from their joined hands into his face and saw only the solemnity of his expression.

"I'm counting on it."

With great difficulty, Thea pulled her hands from his, turned and walked out of the compartment.

CHAPTER ELEVEN

THEY WERE SERVING TEA AGAIN IN THE PARLOR CAR WHEN THEA returned to it, despite the lateness of the hour. Because of all the excitement, many of the people in first-class had missed dinner due to questioning from the police. Thea thought she heard something about there being a second dinner in the restaurant car. Thanks to Mr. Poyntz, she hadn't eaten her dinner, but she was afraid that eating a meal so late after everything would sit too heavily in her stomach.

Real tea was being served, not the sickeningly sweet hot colored water that Inspector Thayne had tried to pass off to her as tea.

As much as she hated to admit it, he had been right. She was feeling better after drinking it. She took one of the tables for two that had been recently vacated. A waiter came and cleared the old dishes away. He brought out a fresh tea set and scones and biscuits and sweets. The sight of most of the food turned her stomach still, but the tea was piping hot.

Thea poured a small splash of milk in the cup with her tea. It was a habit more than a flavor preference to pour milk in. She didn't actually prefer the way the tea tasted with it, but she couldn't seem to break the habit. She ignored the sugar. After the cup of hot sugar water, she didn't think she'd be able to stomach anything remotely sweet.

When Thea had prepared it to her liking, she sipped quietly, enjoying the warmth that the beverage provided her. She was still freezing and had taken Inspector Thayne's coat with her when she had left his compartment, though it was large on her.

The tea warmed her hands through the cup. She was tempted to wrap her hands around the teapot, but she could only imagine the looks she'd get if she did that. Thea already saw the looks she was getting for wearing a too-large man's coat. She wondered what they would think if they knew it was Inspector Thayne's.

Thea nibbled at one of the shortbreads. It was plain and it helped to settle her stomach. She knew she needed something to stop the feeling of dread that had been turning it over and over ever since she had discovered the body and abandoned dinner after Mr. Poyntz's interview. The shortbread was a little bland but was exactly what she needed at the moment. The rest of the tray smelled far too nauseating.

She ate two more of them before she waved over one of the waiters. "Excuse me, would you please get me more of these biscuits?" she motioned to the half-eaten one on her plate. "And please remove these?" She pointed at the tiered serving tray.

"Of course, my lady." The man gave a half bow and took the tray. He returned with a smile and, with a flourish, presented a plate of shortbread. "Is there anything else I can get for you, my lady?"

She smiled back at him, the first real smile she had been able to make since this whole ordeal had started. "No, that's all."

The waiter inclined his head and turned away.

It was then that the conductor stepped up to the front of the car. He had a somber look on his face, worse than when he first found out that there was a dead body on the train.

"Ladies and gentlemen, if I could have your attention please," the conductor spoke loudly. "Detective Chief Inspector Stanton from the Leeds City Police has asked that we remain in the station indefinitely. We will try to get moving as soon as possible, though we may be staying in the station overnight. I apologize on behalf of the Great Northern Railway for the inconvenience."

The groans rose up like a roar as he walked towards the back of the car, heading to the observation car. People were whispering in hushed, angry tones, clearly upset about it all.

But Thea didn't complain. This was good. This meant that maybe she could go see Molly before they left. Maybe she'd get some answers from her. Maybe she'd get some answers from somebody. It also gave her a longer chance to find the killer.

THEA WAS MORE SURPRISED THAN SHE SHOULD HAVE BEEN WHEN Mr. Poyntz found her again in the parlor. She was still leisurely sipping her tea, watching the discord that had erupted after the conductor's announcement.

"So how did it go with Inspector Thayne?" he asked, slipping into the chair across from her and helping himself to a biscuit.

She forced down a gasp.

"Mr. Poyntz! How did you-?"

"I'm a reporter, my lady. It's my job to know these things." Thea fought the scowl that was threatening to show. "So, what did he say?"

Thea frowned, trying but failing to recall what exactly they had been talking about before she had gone to speak with Inspector Thayne. "About?"

"Are the police still looking for suspects?"

Ah. That. Thea gave him the most charming smile she could muster up. "I'm afraid I could hardly presume to speak for the Leeds City Police."

Mr. Poyntz chuckled and reached for a second biscuit. "How very diplomatic of you, my lady. Have you ever thought of a career in politics?"

Thea rolled her eyes.

"Was there something you actually wanted, Mr. Poyntz?"

He shook his head. "No. It was more about what I could do for you." He held up his notebook. "I've spoken to nearly every person in first-class. I figure someone as determined as you would like to hear about the interviews."

Thea swallowed. "How do you know what I might want?"

"Because you and I are cut from the same cloth. If that was my friend being accused of murder, I'd move Heaven and Earth to help them be cleared." He flipped several pages into the notebook. "There were a number of people who all alibied each other out, mostly in the restaurant and parlor car. There was a bridge game going on in the parlor. Mrs. St. John was having an argument in the corridor with Mrs. Beauvale, which was the car in front of yours. Mrs. Beauvale didn't see anyone pass them, other than Mrs. St. John's daughter Nora, who went to the lavatory and returned immediately according to her mother."

Thea's brow furrowed as she tried to digest the information. He had given her so much of it that she had no idea what to make of it. "So what you're saying is that the murderer couldn't have come from farther forward in the train. They had to come from first-class."

Mr. Poyntz grinned like he was proud of her. It was an odd thing to feel from a stranger. "Exactly."

"Which doesn't exactly clear Molly."

"No, but it does eliminate the rest of the train, including several of the staff." He leaned in, whispering conspiratorially. "With a murder investigation, the first thing you want to do is narrow down the pool of who could have done it." He held up the list. "While they could have lied, most people don't usually lie about where they were when someone gets killed. Not unless they have something to hide, that is."

"But how do you find out if they're hiding something because they're the murderer or if they just have secrets?"

He shrugged. "By investigating. Research. Most of my work involves verifying that a source hasn't made up a story for their few moments of fame."

Thea grimaced. She hadn't even considered that. She had been thinking more along the lines of the usual scandals that the aristocracy had to hide.

"From what I saw, it seemed like Mr. Talbot put up quite the fight. I saw blood outside the compartment. Unless, of course, that was from you or your maid?"

She shook her head. "It wasn't."

"Do you think that the killer might have been injured during the fight?"

"I hadn't given it any thought," she lied.

She had suspected that, but it was nice to know that someone else thought the same. It explained the blood on the floor outside the door.

Mr. Poyntz had to have gotten close to see it, since the police hadn't allowed anyone back towards her compartment. Molly hadn't been injured, that she had seen anyway, so the blood couldn't have been hers. It wasn't as if there was a pool of blood by Mr. Talbot's body for her or the killer to step in, so it had to be the killer's blood.

"Since you are asking questions anyway, would you mind asking if anyone saw Molly?"

Mr. Poyntz chuckled. "I do believe you just answered my first question, Lady Theodora."

Thea blinked and swallowed. She figured the best thing she could do was pretend to be ignorant. "Which question was that again?"

The reporter raised his brow. "If I truly believed that you don't remember, I wouldn't be here talking to you." He stood up, bowing his head to her. "And on that note, I'm going to retire now."

He left his notebook behind on the table. Somehow, Thea doubted it was an accident.

CHAPTER TWELVE

THEA FOUND IT HARD TO BELIEVE THAT THE TRAIN WOULD BE stopped at York indefinitely. The rails worked on a schedule. If she was a betting woman, she would say that they'd be moving again before the next day was over.

Lacking any place to stay for the night, Thea claimed one of the many empty chairs in the observation car. While many of the passengers were too unnerved to sleep, the observation car was almost empty, other than the few others who had been displaced from her compartment's car, so she had her choice of seats.

She still had Mr. Poyntz's notebook and had flipped through it a number of times. There had to be some clue in it that she was missing, but she wasn't sure what that was yet. After the day she had been through, Thea had started to doze when Mrs. Livingston came into the car. She was looking around rather purposefully and when she caught a glimpse of Thea, she walked towards her.

"I couldn't help but overhear before," Mrs. Livingston started. She sat down beside Thea. "When you were in Inspector Thayne's compartment," the other woman clarified. Thea couldn't help but roll her eyes. Of course the elegant, brightly clad woman had been eavesdropping. She was hardly surprised. "Do you really believe your maid is innocent?"

Thea ground her jaw tightly. She should have figured that the other woman would bring that up again. It seemed to be all anyone wanted to talk about. "Yes, I do. Molly wouldn't hurt a fly."

The American woman nodded, dropping gracefully into the chair next to her. Thea couldn't help but envy her a little. She always felt so clumsy and awkward, especially compared to the more dignified women who frequented the upper class.

"I would like to offer my help, whatever I can do."

Mrs. Livingston's accent had dropped from her voice, as if she had forgotten to use it or had given up her pretext of being a southern belle. Her words carried the more refined pronunciation of the American upper class.

"You think she's innocent then?" Thea asked in confusion. She hadn't thought that anyone outside of her, Inspector Thayne, and perhaps Mr. Poyntz thought so.

Mrs. Livingston nodded enthusiastically. "I would be more than happy to do what I can to help clear that poor girl's name, no matter how long it takes."

"I thought you had a house party to attend," Thea probed as carefully as she could.

Mrs. Livingston scoffed. "I'll be arriving late as it is, but I'm sure my hosts won't mind much. They wouldn't mind if I didn't show up at all."

The American muttered the last sentence to herself. Thea relaxed a bit at hearing it. It seemed that there was much more to Mrs. Livingston than her first impression. She found this version much more pleasant and felt as if she had much more in common with this one.

"Since you aren't allowed to return to your compartment, I

would like to offer mine. You shouldn't have to sleep in a chair."

Thea gave a small smile, feeling immensely grateful. "That's very kind of you to do that for me, Mrs. Livingston. We only just met."

Mrs. Livingston grinned largely, her teeth showing as she did. "Us girls have to stick together. And it's Wilhelmina, darling."

"Thea," she said in return, finally giving into this woman.

Thea figured that if she was going to spend the remainder of the journey in Wilhelmina's compartment, they might as well be on a first name basis with each other. Especially if the American woman was determined to help her find the real killer. Thea might actually like her, now that Wilhelmina wasn't pretending to be as obnoxious as she had been.

Wilhelmina sat down in the chair beside her. "There is one thing I would ask of you in return." Thea cocked her head as she waited for the other woman to continue. "I had a brooch locked in my compartment. My husband gave it to me, you see, so I had packed it when I thought he would be coming with me. It's a family heirloom, so I imagine he would be rather angry to discover that someone has stolen it."

"Do you have any idea who?"

Wilhelmina shook her head. "I'm afraid not. I never took it out of my compartment."

"Do you think it's the same person who took Mr. Worsley's watch and Mrs. Beauvale's pearls?"

"Perhaps," Wilhelmina said before she leaned in conspiratorially. "Mrs. Beauvale thought she caught Mrs. St. John in the act as she was coming out of her compartment, but it turned out that Mrs. St. John was just another victim of our thief. She saw Mrs. Beauvale's compartment door had been left open and went to make sure everything was alright."

"That's unbelievable. So there are no leads?"

Wilhelmina shook her head. "None. Speaking of, do we have any suspicions on who might have killed Mr. Talbot?"

"Not really," Thea lied as she tucked the notebook back inside her purse, not wanting to give too much away yet.

Just because Wilhelmina had volunteered to help didn't mean she couldn't be guilty. For all Thea knew, this woman could be the killer or in league with them. Wilhelmina had left earlier than Inspector Thayne and her. She hadn't ruled anyone else out as a suspect yet.

Well, not everyone. There were a number of people who had been cleared by Mr. Poyntz's notes, people who had been in the observation, lounge, and parlor. She was amazed by the amount he had spoken to, though he had to be used to interviewing people so efficiently from his work. There had also been a number of passengers who had remained in the restaurant car after Thea had left.

"Do you think it's possible the thief did it?"

"It's possible." The other woman pursed her lips, gesturing to a steward. "Will you please get me a pen and some paper?"

The boy bobbed. "Of course, ma'am."

He returned a few minutes later with some stationery and a pen. Wilhelmina smiled charmingly at the young man.

"Why thank you ever so much," she drawled. He blushed and scampered off, heading towards the front of the car. She turned her attention back to Thea. "Well don't you worry now. I've read every work by Edgar Allen Poe and all of the Sherlock Holmes books. We'll solve this thing in no time."

Thea wasn't sure that made her feel entirely secure, but perhaps Wilhelmina would be useful.

"I'm going to make a list of everyone on this side of the train who couldn't have done it. There were the four of us, the waiters, and the head waiter. There was also a gentleman who was sitting a few tables away and—" she cut off suddenly. "Did you see a woman leave the dining car?"

Thea's head popped up. Until that point, she had started to tune out the American woman's musings. "What did you say?"

"There was a woman at lunch. She was wearing a dark red suit. She left the dining car mid-meal."

"I saw her," Thea said carefully, "What about her?"

"Well, when she came back, she was wearing a dress. I doubt very many people noticed, but well, clothing is a passion of mine. It struck me as odd that she had changed clothes then. Why put on a dress in the middle of lunch?"

She had also wondered but had mostly forgotten about the woman until Wilhelmina brought her up again. She let out a breath of relief, closing her eyes to offer up a silent prayer of thanks. "You saw that too!"

"Of course. I also thought it was strange because who brings extra clothes into their compartment?" Wilhelmina glanced down at her suit mourningly. "I wish I had. Mine's all in the baggage car." Thea nodded. Her trunk was there too. "Do you think we should tell the police about the woman?"

Thea shook her head. "I don't think the police would take us seriously. Do you?" She sighed out loud. "I can hear them now. 'So what that a woman changed her dress? Perhaps she spilt food on her clothes. Leave the detecting to the professionals.'"

Wilhelmina frowned.

"Yes, well, you're right about that," she sighed heavily. The American had all but given up on her original accent, the one she had in the restaurant car, settling into the other one. She too was not what she had appeared to be. She, like so many of the others around Thea, had been lying about herself.

"I do have to ask you something," Thea said, trying to figure out how to tactfully broach the subject. Tact had never been her forte, much to her mother's chagrin.

"What is it about?" the other woman asked softly.

"Your accent. It's changed from earlier."

Wilhelmina closed her eyes, shoulders drooping in defeat. She sighed heavily, as if the weight of the world had been dropped on her shoulders.

"Mr. Livingston's first wife was from San Antonio, Texas. He loved her very much." She suddenly looked much older. "He didn't want a new wife. He wanted a replacement for her."

"Replacement?"

"She passed away not long before he met my father. My father is in the oil business and Mr. Livingston has made a few investments." Wilhelmina sighed heavily. "It doesn't help that my father is from Texas, so Mr. Livingston assumed I was as well."

"You aren't?" Thea asked. She hadn't paid much attention to the United States or any of their many states. She knew her mother was from Chicago and her parents had a cottage in a place called Newport.

Wilhelmina shook her head. "I grew up with my grandmother in Rhode Island. My father didn't know what to do with me after my mother died, so my grandmother took me in."

"The accent you had earlier wasn't real?" Thea prompted.

"Mr. Livingston hired a phonetics teacher to give me lessons on how to speak 'like a good little Texas belle.'" Her words twanged in the overdramatic accent. Wilhelmina glared out the window. "He even hired his first wife's lady's maid to ensure I look the same as she did."

Thea swallowed hard. The thought of someone going to those lengths was sickening. Some of the rituals surrounding mourning seemed excessive, but that was another extreme.

"Your father arranged the marriage to help his business then?" Thea asked, despite how rude of a question it was.

Wilhelmina shook her head, keeping her back still to Thea. "My step-mother brought me. She wanted me to marry well.

She said that a titled husband would give me many opportunities in life." She laughed, but it was humorless and hollow. "She had my best interests in heart. And when Mr. Livingston proposed, I thought I was so lucky. The heir to a viscounty wanted me."

That made sense. So many rich American women had come in search of a titled husband and those titled men were in search of a rich wife to help save their estates. Million-dollar princesses, she had heard them called. They were wealthy beyond belief and they were the salvation to many British lords' financial problems.

That had been the case for her mother and father. The Prescott-Pryce family had a long history of not doing the best job to hold on to their money. The Craven fortune had been the answer to her father's money troubles. It had only been luck that her parents had loved each other.

"So what happened?"

"It turned out that Mr. Livingston had just recognized my name. My inheritance and dowry were both in shares to my father's oil business. He was only after my money. He found it to be a bonus that I looked like his first wife and I was too timid to say no to his attempts to mold me into her."

Thea actually felt bad for the woman. It was such a horrible story, but unfortunately common. So many of the American heiresses had come over thinking they would find themselves in a fairytale only to be trapped in loveless marriages. Some were downright miserable. There were so few like her parents.

"Sometimes, I wish he was dead," the American woman said quietly, almost too low for Thea to hear her. Her voice was like a prayer, her face tilted upwards. "Lord, I wish he had been here, instead of the poor chap in your compartment."

Thea swallowed. It was a horrible thing to say, but she could hardly blame her. He sounded like a cold man, uncaring.

"I've looked into divorce," Wilhelmina spoke again, her voice a little louder this time, "but without a good reason, I'm unlikely to ever be granted one."

Thea's heart went out to the American as she dropped her head into her hands. She shook slightly and Thea wondered if she would cry. But Wilhelmina's face was dry when she pulled back to stare at Thea.

"What you must think of me?" she whispered, "I sound so selfish. I should be grateful! But I'm not." She sounded terribly bitter. "I hate him," Wilhelmina spat with more passion than she had displayed about anything, a fair amount of anger mixed into her voice.

"If I thought that you should be grateful to someone so controlling, I probably would have been married already," Thea stated dryly.

The American woman laughed, but it was borderline hysterical. After a moment, she collected herself.

"We should adjourn to my compartment for the night and get some rest. I have a feeling we'll need it in the morning."

With all that had gone on during the day, it was no wonder that Thea was having a hard time going to sleep. She tossed and turned restlessly, trying to get comfortable in her traveling clothes. Her corset was far too tight to relax in, but without a maid, she didn't dare try to take it off.

Wilhelmina had been kind enough to offer her compartment for Thea to sleep in, but she was having trouble shutting her eyes. Every time she closed them, all she could picture was Mr. Talbot's body. His blood everywhere. His hands and nails coated red from where he had fought for his life. The hatpin won during the struggle. Mr. Talbot had done his best to tell them who had killed him. In his last moments, he had tried to give them everything they might have needed to solve the case. The fact that none of the clues lined up frustrated Thea.

She pulled out Mr. Poyntz's notebook from where she'd tucked it. The moonlight and artificial lights from outside were barely enough to make out the words on the page, but she didn't dare go into the hallway. The killer was still on the loose. She didn't want those notes to fall into their hands.

Wilhelmina had left the list that she had been working on sitting on the table between them. Thea took a piece of the stationery from the pile and set the notebook beside it. She knew she was going to have to return the book eventually, but she wanted her own copy of the relevant notes.

Thea looked up as Wilhelmina snored quietly, shifting in her sleep. She envied the American woman. Wilhelmina adapted so easily to every situation, taking everything in stride. Thea doubted that most people would jump at the chance to help investigate a murder. Until Molly had been arrested, Thea had been content to stay away from the whole affair. But she was invested in finding the real killer now.

"Thea?" Wilhelmina asked groggily as she turned over.

Thea snatched the notebook off the table, slipping it back into her purse.

"What are you doing up still?" the woman asked, sitting up as she did.

"Nothing. Just can't sleep."

"Do you want to talk about it?"

Thea shook her head, curling back up on the seat. "No. I'll try to sleep again." Through the moonlight, she could barely make out the woman's unconvinced expression. "Goodnight, Wilhelmina."

The American watched her for another minute before she decided that Thea was being genuine. She turned back over and seemed to go back to sleep.

Not wanting to get caught again, Thea did the same.

CHAPTER THIRTEEN

THE RESTAURANT CAR WASN'T NEARLY AS CROWDED FOR breakfast as Thea had expected it to be. It was early and many people were still sleeping. Wilhelmina had simply turned over and grumbled when Thea had told her where she was going.

Among the faces in the car, Thea recognized most of them as the passengers who had been displaced by the sleeper being closed off.

A full English breakfast was being served, but Thea was still feeling the effects of the day before. She ordered toast and coffee and was nibbling at the toast when she saw a pair of feet stop before her table.

Mr. Poyntz stood in the aisle, his hand outstretched as if he was expecting something.

"Can I help you, Mr. Poyntz?" she asked sweetly.

"My notebook, Lady Theodora, if you please."

"And who says I have it?"

The look on his face made it clear that the journalist didn't believe her. She sighed, reaching into her purse and extracting the object in question.

"I trust you took any information you deemed would be helpful to your investigation."

"Yes. Thank you."

"I didn't do anything, my lady. I'm a journalist. I report the news. I don't make it."

From the way Mr. Poyntz said it, he had repeated this statement a number of times before. It didn't seem to make it true.

"If you say so."

Mr. Poyntz shook his head. "If you will excuse me, my lady."

He bowed slightly and walked away, as abrupt as ever.

It was only another moment before Inspector Thayne walked into the car, heading directly towards her. Thea was beginning to think he had some sort of way to track her, a sort of mental connection she didn't know about. He stopped in front of her table and looked at her.

"Lady Thea, may I join you?"

She shrugged. "I guess. It depends."

"On?" he prompted.

"On if you come bearing good news or bad. If it's bad, you'll need to hold off on it. I've had enough bad news from yesterday to last a lifetime. I need a bit of time to recover from it."

He smiled, placing his hand on the back of the chair opposite from her.

"So if I come bearing good news, may I sit?"

"By all means." Thea waved her hand, enforcing her words. Inspector Thayne bowed his head, pulled out the chair, and sat down.

"Did they only bring you toast?" he asked as a waiter came over to take his order.

"I sent the rest of the breakfast away," she explained, as he took the pot and poured himself a cup. He proceeded to add an ungodly amount of sugar into his coffee. Thea cringed. "The smell of it was making me ill."

Inspector Thayne chuckled. "You can't survive on toast alone. You'll turn into sticks and bones and fade away."

"I don't plan on surviving on just toast," she insisted. "There's also shortbread."

The inspector laughed, a grin spreading across his face. It was bright and genuine and made Thea want to smile in return, warming her insides better than the coffee had. But she didn't smile back. She fought the urge.

"So you said you had good news?" Thea prompted, trying to be more business-like and professional. She had a job to do. Now was not the time to be flirting with the handsome policeman, not when Molly's life was on the line.

"I do. I spoke with DCI Stanton. You may speak with Molly, so long as I go with you."

Thea was convinced that Inspector Stanton would refuse to let her see her maid. Surprisingly, he was going to allow her to actually talk to Molly. If Inspector Thayne had to accompany her, so be it. It was the price she was willing to pay.

"When can we go?"

"Whenever you're ready to leave." The waiter arrived with Inspector Thayne's breakfast. He looked at the food almost longingly. "Though may I suggest we finish eating?"

Thea smiled at him.

"Of course. As a detective, you would know best. Far be it from me to get between a man and his meal."

Inspector Thayne scrunched his nose at her words.

Thea poured herself a little more coffee, then indicated the coffee pot to him. He nodded, but didn't speak, having already taken a large bite of his food. She poured him a cup and he thankfully didn't add more sugar to the mix. She couldn't imagine how anyone would be able to calm down after that much sugar.

"Thank you," he said when he swallowed the sausage. "It'll be easier to talk to her once we've finished eating. Your mind will be clearer."

Thea nodded. That made sense. She hadn't been thinking too clearly yesterday, but she definitely felt better now, despite everything.

Thea drank down the cup and took another biscuit, glancing up at him coyly as she did so. Inspector Thayne laughed.

———

THEA WASN'T SURE HOW, BUT SOMEHOW INSPECTOR THAYNE had managed to get her suit jacket and hat from her compartment. She gave him back his coat and went to the lavatory to clean up. By the time she returned, Thea looked reasonably put together again. She wished she could have gotten a change of clothes and a bath.

Inspector Thayne had found them a taxi while Thea had been getting ready. The cabbie was waiting impatiently for her and climbed inside as he saw her approaching.

"Thank you for doing this," Thea said softly to the inspector as she got close.

He smiled, holding his hand out to her. "It's no problem."

He helped her up into the taxi and climbed in behind her. Thea got settled and Inspector Thayne called to the driver that they were good to go. She sat back as far as she could and listened as the engine roared to life and the car vibrated down the bumpy road.

Thea shifted in her seat, glancing out the window.

"Are you alright, Lady Thea?" Inspector Thayne asked, still clearly concerned.

Perhaps he thought that she was going to have a nervous breakdown or another episode after yesterday. But she wasn't.

The dizziness had been replaced by anger and annoyance. They would drive her better than any amount of food or sugar water.

"I'm fine, thank you."

Inspector Thayne raised his eyebrow, seeming unconvinced, but otherwise didn't fight her. After all, why wouldn't Thea be alright? She was in a taxi, instead of on the train that should have been on the way to Edinburgh but was instead stuck in York indefinitely. She was going to visit her maid in prison which was a situation she never imagined in her wildest of dreams.

The cab bumped along the road. They darted between what few other motorcars were on the road and horse-drawn carriages. There were honks from horns, but nowhere near as many as were in London. York seemed relatively quiet in comparison, but still quite loud.

"And you, Inspector? I'm sure this isn't how you hoped to be spending your holiday."

His lips quirked up as he glanced out the window then back at her, eyes twinkling mischievously. "No, but at least the company isn't bad."

Thea looked away, feeling her face heating up. In her limited experience, dealing with charming men never ended well for her. But Inspector Thayne wasn't being charming in that overly practiced way he had before, the way so many in London were. There was an awkwardness about him.

The cab jolted to a stop suddenly and they both were nearly thrown from their seats. The driver slammed on the horn, joining the dozens of others doing the same. Outside, there was screaming and shouting. Thea groaned and Inspector Thayne grimaced.

"I must say, I was looking forward to time in the country," he said, "Away from the noises of the city. Not that I don't love living in London, but sometimes it's just so—" he cut himself off, coloring slightly as he turned his head.

"Overwhelming?" she suggested.

He glanced back at her. "You too?"

"It's why my mother suggested I go stay with my cousins early." He smiled at that.

"I'm afraid mine was only a self-imposed exile." The words were full of bitterness and self-loathing. "Not that it'll be any quieter there. Not with my family."

His words felt far more real than the charming façade he had presented.

Thea giggled softly. So she wasn't the only one who felt that way about visiting family. In polite society, she always felt like she was crazy that she would want to take walks on her own occasionally.

Inspector Thayne colored again, as if realizing what he had said. "I—forgive me. I forgot myself."

"Not at all. I feel the same." She realized what she said didn't make any sense. "I mean, London is just so loud, so big. Sometimes it feels as if it's a living entity that I've been trapped inside and sometimes it feels like freedom. When I escape up north, the last thing I want to do is spend every waking moment with another person. Sometimes it's just nice to be alone."

He gave her a look that was a mix between understanding and awe. Thea had never had anyone look at her that way when she had expressed her feelings before. It made her a little uncomfortable, but it also made her a little warm inside.

Then Thea remembered where they were heading, and she felt ashamed. Here she was complaining about her life when Molly was stuck in a horrible prison. She had forgotten about her maid's much greater misfortune to think only of the things that inconvenienced her in life. Her grandmother was right. How selfish was she?

The cab started moving again and the two of them let out a sigh of relief. She wasn't the only one who had felt trapped in this small moving death machine. It made her feel better that the big, important Scotland Yard inspector felt the same.

Thea glanced out the window as the buildings passed by. Dark clouds moved in the sky and she wondered if it was going to rain before they reached the police station. People shuffled along the sidewalks, moving to their destinations, some with purpose, some in leisure. The taxi began to slow in front of one of the brick buildings until the driver came to a complete stop.

"The Police Headquarters," he called back to them.

Inspector Thayne stood, quickly climbing from the cab. He held out his hand to Thea and helped her down.

CHAPTER FOURTEEN

THE LEEDS POLICE HEADQUARTERS building was impressive. It was a decent-sized building, made of brick and stone. It wasn't nearly as awe-inspiring as she remembered Scotland Yard being, but still imposing in its own right.

Uniformed men patrolled the area. Automobiles had been parked outside the building. Thea assumed they were probably used by the police.

Someone in the street drove their cart through a muddy puddle and nearly splashed water on her as the taxi pulled away. Thea moved out of the way in the nick of time. Inspector Thayne hadn't seen the water and cast her an odd look as she jumped. He offered her his arm, and Thea took it.

"Stay close to me, my lady, and you should be alright. Let me do the talking," he ordered gently. His words were spoken near her ear.

Thea shivered and turned her head. The inspector was biting his cheek, repressing a smile. He seemed to know what he was doing to her. She pressed her lips together to keep any emotion from showing. She knew she was attracted to him, but now was not the time or place for such matters.

Thea nodded. "Of course, Inspector. You do know best."

She was trusting him to keep her safe. It was a strange feeling, since she had never needed to rely on anyone that way before. She had put her life into his hands. Thea swallowed hard with the realization. She wasn't used to such feelings.

Inspector Thayne held the door open for her and Thea walked inside. There was a small, cramped reception area in front, with a few chairs for people to wait. Behind the desk led to a darkened hallway. That seemed to be where they kept the criminals. It was probably down that hallway where Molly was being kept.

Thea took in a deep breath and Inspector Thayne put a reassuring hand on her back, before he seemed to realize what he had done, and he withdrew it.

"Sorry," he murmured.

"Don't be," she whispered back.

Inspector Thayne glanced down at her, almost shocked at her words. Thea wasn't sure if he kept doing all those little things on purpose or if it was something he did with every woman he encountered. His reaction made her think this wasn't an everyday occurrence for him.

"Can I help you, miss?" a voice called. A young sergeant, dressed much like Constable Cooke had been, stepped out from around the corner. "Sir?" he implored.

"Yes," Inspector Thayne said, stepping up. "I am Detective Inspector Thayne from Scotland Yard. I spoke with Chief Inspector Stanton earlier about stopping by to question a suspect."

The sergeant snapped to attention.

"Yes, of course, sir," the man all but saluted. It seemed like the uniformed police in Yorkshire were eager to serve. "And the lady, sir?"

"The lady will accompany me."

"Yes, of course, sir," the sergeant said again. "May I get

DCI Stanton for you? He's questioning a suspect now, but if he's expecting you I'm sure—"

"Please," Inspector Thayne said, holding up a hand to stop the other man, "We don't want to be any trouble."

"Oh no, sir, it's no trouble at all."

Thea didn't think that would be the case at all. It wouldn't be any trouble for this officer. However, interrupting DCI Stanton in the middle of his interrogation would make the inspector more unpleasant than he already was, she assumed.

"Sergeant," Thea spoke up, ignoring Inspector Thayne's glare. "Please don't disturb the inspector. We're in no hurry and can wait. Just please let him know as soon as he is free that we are waiting for him."

"Of course, miss."

Thea took Inspector Thayne's arm, curling her fingers around it as tightly as she could and tugged on his coat. She led him towards the chairs firmly. She knew he wasn't happy. She could see it in his very expression.

"I thought I told you to let me do the talking," he hissed once they sat down.

She gave him the dirtiest look she could muster up, not daring to look at him directly. He sounded quite angry. It wouldn't do to make him too angry at her, but at the same time, she couldn't help it. It was like a defense mechanism, to speak sarcastically whenever someone was angry at her.

"Yes and that was going so very well for you," she spat out, "The last thing Molly needs is DCI Stanton being annoyed with us and taking it out on her."

Inspector Thayne shook his head, as if her accusation offended him personally.

"He wouldn't do that," Inspector Thayne protested. "He's an officer of the law."

Thea raised an eyebrow and he seemed to realize what he had said. Inspector Thayne didn't know what kind of man

Inspector Stanton was and it was incredibly naïve for him to assume anything about his character. He sunk back down into his seat, looking defeated. Thea fought back a triumphant smirk, knowing it wouldn't go over well. She didn't need to offend the only policeman who was on her side.

"We don't want to get on his bad side any more than we already are," she murmured, unable to help herself. Inspector Thayne conceded that point, and he nodded solemnly. His fingers found hers and he gripped them solidly. The contact thrilled her, even through her gloves.

"You're a good person, Lady Thea, to be so worried about your friend."

Thea inhaled sharply, fighting the sudden urge to cry. He squeezed her hand tightly for a brief moment before he released it. She pulled her hand back into her own lap. She wished that he had held onto her hand. Her nerves seemed much calmer when he was touching her.

THEA STARTED TO DOZE OFF BY THE TIME THAT DCI STANTON finally showed his face. She could hear the older inspector talking to the desk sergeant as the two came around the corner. Their voices carried loudly, but Thea supposed that was because they didn't expect anyone to fall asleep in the waiting area of the police station. It was the last place she had expected to have been napping.

It seemed that the stress of the day before had taken a toll on her. Her head had come to rest on Inspector Thayne's shoulder as she napped, and she had been surprisingly comfortable. Thea blushed as she glanced over at him. She had never touched a man so familiarly before.

Thea nudged Inspector Thayne lightly with her elbow. He too had fallen asleep. He grunted and straightened up just as

Stanton and the desk sergeant turned the corner into the reception area.

Thea rose to her feet as the inspector approached them. The older man didn't seem thrilled to see them there. She wondered if he hadn't expected them to actually show up.

"Chief Inspector Stanton," Inspector Thayne greeted, standing up and offering his hand, "thank you for meeting with us on such short notice."

The older man gave a grunt, but otherwise didn't reply. He ignored Inspector Thayne's offered hand and Inspector Thayne dropped it awkwardly. The younger man glanced to her and Thea gave a half-hearted shrug.

"Anyway," Inspector Thayne said, trying to soldier through the uncomfortableness, "Would we be able to see Miss Forbes now?"

Inspector Stanton's irritation at them increased in that moment, letting out a heavy sigh as if to tell them that the weight of the world was on his shoulders. Then, he nodded curtly and pursed his lips.

"If you'll just follow me," the other man said. He turned and moved back behind the counter. He plucked a ring of keys off the wall. They clanged loudly in protest, just like everything else in the station.

Thea moved forward as quickly as she could without looking desperate. Inspector Thayne slipped past her and she followed closely behind. She didn't want him to get too far away from her. Thea found herself monitoring her steps so that she didn't trip on his feet or run into his back.

Inspector Stanton and Inspector Thayne stopped suddenly as they came upon a locked room. Thea nearly ran into the younger man, but she managed to halt in time.

Inspector Stanton put one of the keys in the lock and turned. He pushed the door open and looked back at them.

"I can give you one hour with Miss Forbes," he told them, his face rather emotionless.

"Thank you, Inspector," Thea spoke formally and this time, Inspector Thayne didn't glare at her for speaking, "I appreciate it."

CHAPTER FIFTEEN

THEA STEPPED INSIDE THE ROOM, PAST BOTH OF THE MEN. Inspector Thayne followed, closing the door behind them with a resounding thud. Thea shivered with the finality of it.

Molly was more of a mess than she had been the day before. She was still wearing the same bloodstained clothes. Her face had not been washed properly, so the tracks of tears were visible from where they had streamed down her cheeks. The girl was paler than she had been before the police had brought her here. Her hands were shackled to the table and they only served to make her look smaller.

The room was dark and cramped with a low ceiling that if Thea were to reach up, she could almost touch. The air was heavy and hard to breathe. The electric lights were dim, flickering slightly, but Thea was surprised that they worked at all. The gray walls were dirtied and bloodstained. Mold grew on the walls, mostly in the corners. Overall, the room had a damp chill, as if it was underground and not in the back of a police station.

There was a small, grubby window on one wall, but it was positioned in such a way that it couldn't be seen through from the inside. Perhaps it was just a mirror, used to judge a subject's expressions as the police interrogated them. Whatever the purpose the piece of glass served, it was in desperate need of a shine, much like everything else in the cell-like room.

"My lady," Molly whispered in relief, standing up in shock as if Thea was the answer to her prayers. However she had forgotten the shackles and so her arms were bent awkwardly over the table. "My lady, I'm so sorry. I didn't do it."

"I know you didn't," Thea said quietly, moving farther into the room. She was grateful that DCI Stanton had left them to speak with Molly privately. Thea doubted that the man would have allowed this to continue. Inspector Thayne stood back and allowed them this moment uninterrupted. Thea reached for Molly's hands, gripping them tightly with her own as she studied her maid's face. This girl was the closest she had ever had to a sister and she hated to see this happening to Molly. "Are you alright?"

Thea winced. That was stupid, insensitive. Of course Molly wasn't alright. The girl had suffered a great loss and then had been arrested. These monsters wouldn't even allow her to clean herself up properly. They wanted her to look guilty, covered in the victim's dried and flaking blood.

"I'm okay, my lady." The girl forced a small smile, but it did little to reassure Thea. Molly's grip on Thea's hands was feeble at best.

"Sit," Thea ordered, before she realized how it sounded, "Please?"

Molly nodded, all but collapsing back into the chair. She looked even more exhausted now than when they had entered the room. Thea swallowed.

"Will you tell us what happened, Miss Forbes?" Inspector Thayne asked her quietly from where he had been watching them. Only now did he approach the table, like Molly was a cornered animal who might start if too many people came at her at once.

"Daniel and I had just been talking, but then I needed to use the lavatory. He said he'd wait in the compartment. I didn't expect Lady Theodora to be back soon from lunch. I was only supposed to be gone a few minutes. If I had known, I never would have left."

"If you hadn't left," Thea spoke up, feeling impassioned, "you might have been dead now too."

"It would be better than a world where I have to live without him," Molly shot back with equal fire, but then deflated as if realizing what she had said and to whom she had said it.

"I'm sure he wouldn't have wanted that for you," she told the other woman. Molly sniffled and Thea pulled her handkerchief out from her purse and handed it to her, before sitting down across from her. The maid wiped her eyes and blew her nose.

"Thank you, my lady," she whispered.

"What delayed you from returning promptly?" Inspector Thayne asked. It was incredible to watch how instantaneously the blood drained from Molly's face.

"I was ill, Inspector." She didn't seem to be lying, but she was avoiding Thea's eyes, as if she was terrified at Thea's judgment.

"Ill?" the inspector repeated, as if he couldn't quite believe that.

Molly stared at the table as if it were deeply fascinating. There was nothing that showed, but somehow Thea knew what the girl was trying to hide, what until that point she had successfully hidden.

"It's Mr. Talbot's, isn't it?" Thea asked as gently as she could. "The baby?"

Molly stared up at Thea in shock. Her eyes watering as she nodded vehemently.

Inspector Thayne appeared greatly embarrassed by this revelation. Thea wondered if Inspector Stanton knew. Somehow, she doubted it.

"Perhaps you should start from the beginning," Inspector Thayne said, coming up to stand behind her.

"We were married, Daniel and I," Molly started softly. "Before I came to work for your family, my lady."

Thea nodded. Molly had admitted that much the day before. Thea figured that this marriage had to have been before Molly came to work for her family, but she found she wasn't angry that Molly never mentioned it before. After all, the maid was entitled to her secrets. She had earned that right. She had helped Thea through the loss of her father and her three bad Seasons.

"It was nearly two weeks before my father found out and had our marriage annulled," Molly continued, "I was fifteen at the time. My father said I was too young. The law agreed with him."

She laughed bitterly.

Thea glanced back at Inspector Thayne. He had an equally confused look on his face. An annulled marriage did not equal a motive for killing him. Thea knew that from what little she knew of murders from reading what few mysteries she had.

"Daniel and I kept in touch, even though our parents did their best to keep us apart."

That sounded like a motive to Thea, but not for Molly to have killed him. Perhaps Molly's parents or even Mr. Talbot's parents who disapproved of the marriage killed him. It did raise the question as to why they would have wanted to keep them apart.

"We were married again in secret on one of my afternoons

off. We didn't tell anyone, because our parents swore to disown us both if we remarried. Our fathers hate each other very much. They were once business partners, before I was born, but something happened." Molly shook her head and clutched the handkerchief in her hand. "I'm afraid I don't know the story."

Thea patted Molly's hand. "That's alright."

"Daniel and I started talking about me giving my notice once we found out about the baby." Her hand cradled against her stomach protectively. "We were going to tell our parents about our marriage when I got back from Scotland."

Thea watched the realization spark in Inspector Thayne's eyes as he followed the movement of Molly's hands.

"Do you know who might have wanted him dead?" Inspector Thayne asked her softly, sitting down next to Thea.

Molly shook her head again. "No, but Daniel had a number of business ventures. He was trying to make his own fortune." Molly put a hand over her mouth as she sobbed. "I always said that he worked too much, that it would wind up killing him."

The pieces clicked together in her head. Molly had come to them when she was sixteen. "Was that why you became a maid? To try to support yourself so he wouldn't have to worry?"

The other woman nodded. "I just wanted to make things easier for him. He is my world and now he's gone. I don't know what I'm going to do."

Molly brought the handkerchief back up to her face, wiping her nose again. Her hand was trembling badly, and she seemed like she was trying her hardest to not start sobbing again. Molly clutched at her stomach like it was a lifeline. Maybe it was, the last piece of her husband that existed.

Thea's heart clenched tightly. Molly had loved Mr. Talbot so much. Mr. Talbot must have loved her to have worked so hard to defy their parents to be together. It also gave the Talbots a surprisingly good motive to want their son dead. If they thought that Mr. Talbot and Molly were close to being together without worrying about him being disowned, they would have lost control over their son completely.

When Molly finally calmed down, she bit her lip uncomfortably. She was clearly debating about something, though Thea didn't know what that might be.

"Inspector Thayne, would you mind turning around?" she asked sheepishly, shifting in her chair.

Inspector Thayne's brow furrowed, but he stood and averted his eyes, turning around so that he didn't see anything. When Molly was satisfied that he wasn't looking, she leaned forward and reached into her blouse. She produced an envelope of considerable size, large enough that Thea was impressed that it had fit. It was about the size of a letter but was bulging as if it was filled with more papers than should have been in there.

Thea inhaled slightly, as she recognized the envelope that the man in question had given Molly while they thought Thea was sleeping. He had said that the envelope shouldn't be dangerous. Yet he was clearly wrong, since he was now dead.

"You can look now, Inspector."

Molly set the envelope on the table. Inspector Thayne turned back, frowning as he spotted the envelope that hadn't been there previously. "Daniel gave me this before. He seemed…" she paused for a second, trying to figure out the right emotion, "…worried. Like he knew somehow." She glanced away, looking like she might burst into tears again. "He knew he was going to die. He just didn't want to worry me."

Molly sniffed and Thea couldn't help but envy her self-control. If she had been in Molly's place, she would be a wreck. She wouldn't have been able to stop herself from sobbing uncontrollably.

"Is that why he gave you the envelope?" Inspector Thayne asked Molly, sitting back down. His arm brushed against Thea's as he reached for the envelope.

"I think so," Molly sniffled. "He told me to give it to the police if anything were to happen to him."

"Why didn't you give it to DCI Stanton?"

It was a valid question. Wouldn't these papers prove her innocence? If Mr. Talbot had given it to her and told her to give it to the police, didn't Molly think that these papers should be able to clear her. They might have even named the real killer. If that was the case, then it would be as Molly had said. Mr. Talbot had known that he was going to die.

"I don't trust him. He scares me." Molly inhaled sharply. "He's so sure that I am guilty, and I don't understand why."

Thea nodded understandingly and Inspector Thayne held his hand across the table. "May I see them?" he asked, indicating the envelope.

Molly nodded, handing it to him. The inspector popped the seal open and pulled the papers out. A few were crinkled, as if they had been stuffed into the envelope in haste. Inspector Thayne flipped through them quickly. He frowned as he reached the end and began looking through them again, slower this time. He studied them for the reason why Mr. Talbot might have told Molly to hide them, his expression growing darker with each second that passed.

"I can see why he asked you to give these to the police," he said carefully, still looking through the papers. "I only wonder why he didn't bring these to the police himself."

Molly shook her head. "That wasn't like Daniel. He didn't like to ask for help. He didn't want to accuse someone of doing something without proof."

Inspector Thayne looked up at her, eyes wide and expression serious. "Do you know what's in these papers?"

A confused look spread over Molly's face. She shook her head, very adamantly. "No, I didn't look at them. I figured they must have been evidence against someone. Why else would he be so upset?"

Inspector Thayne placed the papers down on the table. He turned them so that Thea and Molly could see them.

Thea leaned in, reading as quickly as she could. On the top, there was a name of a business, a fairly well-known department store, Fletcher's, near the center of London. It was newer, but she had shopped there before. She had a shawl and a hat that she had bought from there. The store sold good quality items for being prêt-à-porter and had never had anyone say anything about the items when she had worn them.

Underneath was a list of what looked like account numbers and money. Accounting papers. They had been marked up with notes in the margins. Some of the numbers had been circled.

Mr. Talbot had taken accounting papers from Fletcher's. He must have thought someone was stealing from Fletcher's. These papers weren't the kind of thing the general public would have access to.

"It's lucky that you kept these on you. The killer would have found them quite valuable, I think." He paused as Thea kept staring at the papers from where they lay. "How did he get these?" Inspector Thayne asked, as if reading Thea's mind.

"Daniel's one of the founding partners. He's on the board of directors. His roommate from Eton, Lionel Fletcher, founded it with him. They decided that Daniel would not be the public face, since he was also in law."

"So he would have had access to all of the financial records?" Thea asked, beating Inspector Thayne to the question this time. He looked up at her, almost like he was shocked that she had spoken before he could.

"Yes, of course."

Inspector Thayne's frown deepened as he moved the papers. "Did Mr. Talbot ever mention to you that he suspected money was going missing from Fletcher's, money that should have been there, but wasn't?"

Molly shook her head. "No. He doesn't—didn't really like to talk business with me when we're together. Our time is always so short." She shifted in her chair, playing with the handkerchief. "He did mention something about some inconsistencies at work. But I thought he was talking about at the firm."

"Firm?"

Molly nodded. "Daniel works as a solicitor at his father's law firm. It was formed when his father and my father split the firm. His father wanted him to take over. That's why Daniel wanted to keep his name off of the department store. He didn't want his father interfering." She glanced down, staring at the papers. Thea reached for them, looking through them, "I think he was always afraid his father would make him quit the store. But Daniel planned to hand in his notice to the law firm soon."

"Did his father know that he was quitting the firm?"

Molly's eyes widened. "He might have." She snapped her fingers, remembering something suddenly. "Daniel had mentioned something about gambling debts. But they weren't his. Daniel didn't gamble. He hated wasting money and he felt that gambling was a waste unless he knew he would win." She frowned, thinking on it. "I think Lionel might have. I remember playing bridge against him. He was very competitive."

"Lionel?"

"Lionel Fletcher. He was Daniel's partner."

Thea stared. The margins were filled with scrawled notes about stolen money, about how there were too many inconsistencies. Mr. Talbot certainly hadn't meant at the law firm. He had to have meant all the inconsistencies in the accounting books. Mr. Talbot thought someone was stealing money, that much was obvious by the notes in the margins of the papers.

Someone at Fletcher's was stealing money, funneling out large amounts of money in little batches. Mr. Talbot had found out who that someone was, and they probably knew that he knew. If that wasn't a motive to kill someone, Thea wasn't sure what was. After all, what better reason was there to murder than love or money?

"Do you know if Mr. Talbot thought someone was stealing money from Fletcher's?" Thea blurted out, interrupting whatever Inspector Thayne and Molly had been talking about.

The two of them turned to stare incredulously at her. Thea bit her lip. She hadn't meant to cut in. Sometimes she just got so absorbed into her own mind that she didn't pay attention to what was going on around her.

"Why do you ask?" Inspector Thayne was looking at her with an intensity that startled her.

"Molly mentioned inconsistencies and it's all here in the papers." Thea motioned to the various spots on the pages, flipping between them as she pointed at the different erratic variables. "Someone was channeling money out. Wouldn't that give them motive to kill Daniel, if Daniel had discovered that they were stealing and was going to turn them in to the police once he had more evidence?"

Inspector Thayne grabbed the papers from her, flipping through the pages quickly, scanning each of them. He stopped, staring as he ran his fingers over the words at the bottom page.

"You're right," he said, and Thea felt a little offended at how surprised he sounded. "This does give someone else a motive."

Inspector Thayne rose suddenly, the chair scrapping as he stood up. He folded the papers and tucked them into his jacket pocket.

"What are you doing?" Molly asked nervously, her eyes unbelievably wide. She looked like she wanted to jump across the table and grab the papers from him. Thea understood the urge, she nearly did the same.

"Come on, we're going," Inspector Thayne said to Thea as he headed towards the door.

"What?" Thea all but shouted as she stood. "What do you mean we're going? It hasn't been an hour yet."

He turned to her, looking her right in the eyes. "I need to catch the train back to London and I'm not leaving you here. I'll explain at the station." He looked back to Molly, who was rooted in her chair, frozen in fear. "I'll be back. But in the meantime, don't tell anyone about that envelope." Thea almost snorted and she would have if she wasn't in such a panic. It would have been far more likely for Molly to have taken the secret of the envelope to her grave. She might have done just that if she had been in the compartment when the killer had visited it. He shook his head. "You can't trust anyone here."

Molly inhaled deeply, looking just as terrified as possible. And Thea didn't blame her. If a stranger had told Thea that she was going to stay in prison, she'd be downright terrified too. As it was, Molly was easily the bravest person she knew.

Then Molly closed her eyes and a strange sort of calmness took over her maid's face.

"I understand, Inspector Thayne. Thank you for all your help." She turned to Thea, her eyes pleading. "My lady, I'm so sorry for lying to you about it. Please know that, if I don't get to see you again."

Thea reached out and grasped her maid's hands, squeezing them tightly between hers.

"We will see each other again. I'm going to get you out of

here." Thea gave her a smile, but she didn't believe it herself. "We're going to find the real killer. I'll be back for you soon."

Inspector Thayne knocked on the door before it swung open for them. He offered her his arm and Thea took it, holding it as firmly as she could. She allowed him to lead her out of the interview room, afraid she would bolt back inside it and try to free Molly if she didn't. Thea knew it would only make matters worse for Molly if she did.

CHAPTER SIXTEEN

"Done so soon?" DCI Stanton asked them, almost mockingly. Thea squeezed Inspector Thayne's arm tighter, wanting very much to strike Stanton across his smug face. Inspector Thayne reached his other hand up, resting it over hers and rubbing it gently until she relaxed her grip.

Inspector Thayne nodded. "Yes, I do believe we have all we need."

He smirked at them. "Good. That's excellent."

"Yes. Thank you for all your help, Inspector," Inspector Thayne said, offering his free hand out to shake the other man's. Stanton took it and shook it firmly.

"Are you both heading back now?"

"Yes. Though I'm afraid I've been recalled to London. You know how this line of work is," he said. Thea glanced at him, trying to pretend like she knew about this, like he hadn't sprung this on her.

Constable Cooke came down the hallway whistling. He carried a tray of tea and sandwiches as he headed towards Molly's cell. Inspector Stanton frowned.

"Where are you taking that, Constable?" he asked.

"To Miss Forbes, sir. She hadn't eaten."

The older man seemed like he might protest for a moment, before he remembered that Thea and Inspector Thayne were standing there.

"Very good, Constable. Continue."

The younger man nodded, dipping his head to acknowledge both of them. DCI Stanton unlocked the door and opened it again for the man to enter.

"Well, I'll let you go," he said, turning back to them. "If I have any other questions when I'm finalizing the paperwork, I'll let you know."

Inspector Thayne gave him a curt nod before he turned around and led her out of the police station.

CHAPTER SEVENTEEN

Thea was very proud that she had managed not to ask Inspector Thayne what was going on. She managed not to bother him about it outside of the police station nor in the cab back to the station. She had managed to hold back as they exited the cab and were waiting in line at the ticket booth. Thea didn't even question him as he had bought his ticket for the return train to London.

Thea followed Inspector Thayne back onto the *Flying Scotsman*, trailing behind him into his compartment. Unable to hold back any longer, she slid the door shut behind them. She didn't want to cause a scene.

"Alright, Inspector," she said, crossing her arms over her chest as he pulled his luggage down from the rack, "Please explain to me what is going on. I'm afraid I'm quite lost."

"I think DCI Stanton is trying to frame Molly."

Thea scoffed. "Well obviously! I could have told you that when he kept insisting that hatpin was Molly's."

"What hatpin?" Inspector Thayne asked her, a small frown on his face as the space between his eyes furrowed.

"The one that Mr. Talbot was holding." He slowly nodded,

recognition rising in his eyes. In the next instant, she could see the horror on his face. "When I was questioned by DCI Stanton, he had it as evidence. He tried to trick me into admitting it was one of Molly's, but it was far fancier and gaudier than anything she would have owned."

"Have you taken into consideration that she was married to one of the owners of Fletcher's?" he asked,

Thea frowned, thinking on it, "Yes, but she would have never owned that pin. It wasn't to her tastes. I've been shopping with her before."

Inspector Thayne nodded slowly. "I don't mean it to sound like I'm accusing your maid. There's many details about this case that don't add up."

Thea sat down on the bench. "There was a woman in the dining car that was wearing a hat that it would have matched. She had it on when she left the dining car, but didn't have it on later when she came back in. In fact, she had changed clothes completely when she came back in to finish lunch."

"I saw her." Inspector Thayne frowned, clearly puzzled. A thoughtful expression passed over his face. "You noticed that?"

"It was rather strange. No one changes their clothing in the middle of lunch. Not unless there was very important reason for it."

Inspector Thayne stared at her openly for a minute, before he shook his head in disbelief. He almost seemed to be laughing at her.

"What?" Thea asked.

"You noticed something so simple, something so obvious, that most people would miss completely. I didn't even pay attention to that she had changed her clothing until you mentioned it now. I did see the woman you were talking about though. She had quite the hat."

Thea smiled, feeling proud about that and then laughing at the thought. It had been quite an impressive hat. Then she frowned. "Why are you rushing back to London, if you think Molly is innocent and Stanton is framing her?"

"I can't do anything about it here. I don't have any evidence against him, and I have no connections here to help me. However, these papers are evidence against someone in Fletcher's. I was going to try talking to Lionel Fletcher. Perhaps I can get some answers in London." Thea was sure the frown on her face must have been obvious, because Inspector Thayne gave her a small smile. "Don't look so worried. I'll be back here as soon as I can. The sooner I get answers, the sooner we can have Molly freed from prison."

Thea extended her hand to him, determined to act as properly and formally as possible, in case this was the last time they met. She didn't want Inspector Thayne's impression of her to be that of a flighty debutant, throwing herself at any man that came close. She had been so relaxed with him that even her open-minded American mother would have had a fit. "Well then, Inspector, I do wish you the best of luck in your search."

Inspector Thayne smiled again, larger this time. He took her hand gently, turning it in his as he bowed at the waist and kissed her knuckles. A thrill ran through her spine. "Until we meet again, Lady Thea."

CHAPTER EIGHTEEN

THEA FELT STRANGELY DESPONDENT AFTER INSPECTOR Thayne's departure. Without him there, what more could she do to help Molly? Despite having been to the police station, she was feeling rather restless. To try to combat these feelings, Thea had sought solace in the observation car.

That was where Wilhelmina found her, curled into a chair and watching out the back as other trains came and left the station.

"Did you have a productive trip?" the American asked as she approached.

"I did, thank you." Thea looked up at her and set the stack of papers in her hand.

"I finished my list of everyone I saw and where they were."

Wilhelmina held the papers out to Thea. As she flipped through, Thea was surprised at the detail and care that had gone into them. She hadn't noticed half of the people listed, so she was astonished at the amount of work that the American woman had put into them for a complete stranger.

Most of the people were described by clothing, some by their features.

"We should talk to them. We can divide up the list and see where people were and who they saw."

Thea nodded. "That sounds like a good idea. How did you remember all of these people?"

Thea wasn't sure how Wilhelmina managed to keep track of them all, nor how she could remember the amount of detail about them that she did. From her descriptions, it was easy to identify each person without their names. When she got away from the American, she would run through her list that she had taken from Mr. Poyntz.

Wilhelmina waved one of the papers. "There was a game I used to play with some of my friends back in the States. We used to try to guess who had designed the clothes or where they had them made."

"How often were you right?"

She laughed softly, melodiously. "Not as often as I'd like, but I also wasn't wrong as much as the others were."

Thea smiled. She could almost just imagine the happy childhood the other woman must have had. She probably had many friends. Thea could picture them flirting around fashionable society, giggling as they pointed and guessed about various people.

"When I got older, I discovered that I couldn't drown out my thoughts with the sound of my own voice. My mind was always going and the only time it was quiet was when I was watching people. So I got very good at remembering everyone I'd seen."

Wilhelmina had a pleasant voice to listen to, when she wasn't speaking with that obnoxious, over-dramatic accent. It was almost but wasn't quite British. It sounded more like her mother's accent. She still did some over-exaggerated hand gestures, waving her hands with nearly every word she said, it seemed. Thea would almost say that the American was talking with her hands.

"Anyway, I found out who most of the dining car staff were or the others on my way to the observation car. I tried to make a note of where I saw them, but I'm sure I missed some and confused others. But one of them had to have seen someone or something. If Molly was in the washroom, someone must have seen her go in and leave, right?"

"Wouldn't Molly have immediately said that she had seen someone in the hall and that they had seen her before the murder?" Thea pointed out.

Wilhelmina shook her head. She looked a tad bit smug.

"Not necessarily. After all, she might not have seen them. Not everyone would come forward. They probably wouldn't want to be involved. Same was with how no one has come forward with any information about whoever did kill that man."

"Mr. Talbot," Thea corrected automatically.

"Hmm?" the other woman questioned. If she wondered why Thea would say a random name, she said nothing.

"The man who died. His name was Daniel Talbot. He was Molly's husband. Apparently, he owned Fletcher's."

"The department store?" the American woman asked, shocked as Thea nodded. "But he was so young!"

Molly had mentioned that he was older than her, but Thea hadn't really noticed before now. Mr. Talbot had probably only been a year or two older than Thea, but around the same age as Wilhelmina.

"I know," Thea said softly, wondering if the other woman realized that the murdered man had been her age. "It's quite surprising."

"Yes, truly."

"I wonder what will happen to the store now?" Thea pondered out loud.

"I assume that his partner will be taking it over. Wasn't it Lionel Fletcher who owns the store?" Wilhelmina said, glancing back down at her list, "Unless the partner killed him to take control of the business."

The other woman said it so calmly that for a moment, Thea wondered what kind of lives they lived over in America. It was strange how unfazed Wilhelmina seemed about the events of the previous day. Thea didn't think that Wilhelmina could be so untroubled if she had killed Mr. Talbot.

Thea could feel the eyes on her back before she heard the voice from behind. Thea turned sharply to see who it was, and Wilhelmina's eyes bulged.

"Uh, excuse me, my lady," the timid voice came.

Constable Cooke stood there, looking as nervous as he sounded. He shifted awkwardly where he stood. If he was trying to look natural, then he was failing spectacularly. Thea couldn't tell if it was genuine or an act. Both sides had seemed so real. It seemed as if everyone had false identities on this trip, so Thea refused to be surprised if the young constable turned out to be not who he said he was.

"Constable," Thea greeted, unfolding herself from the chair as she stood up to look him in the eyes. "Is there something I can help you with?"

"Actually, my lady, I'm here to help you." He fidgeted a little again, playing with his hands as if he didn't know what to do with them. "DCI Stanton is going to release the train, but the car that your compartment is in is being detached, so I'm here to escort you to gather your belongings from it. I've been working through the car."

Thea smiled, but it felt more like a grimace. "Thank you, Constable. I appreciate it."

"If you would follow me, please."

Thea nodded, but turned back to Wilhelmina. "Would you mind if I put my things in your compartment?"

"No, of course not, darling," the American woman said,

lifting her head back up and straightening herself out. She pulled the key from her purse and handed it to Thea.

Thea smiled gratefully in return, before she turned around and looked at Constable Cooke. "Lead the way, Constable."

"Yes, of course, my lady."

The constable stumbled slightly as he pivoted, tripping over his own feet. Wilhelmina seemed amused, her eyes sparkling as she laughed silently. It would have been rude to laugh out loud about another.

The poor man couldn't help it if he was clumsy, if he was awkward and afraid of his own shadow, even if he was a police officer working on a homicide with a potentially dangerous killer on the loose. If Constable Cooke was just pretending that he was that way, then he was a brilliant actor and deserved to be on stage and not working as a Constable.

Thea hid her own smirk by pressing her lips tightly together.

"I wanted to ask you," Constable Cooke started as they walked, "was Miss Forbes, I mean, Mrs. Talbot sick before you left?"

Thea glanced up at him, trying to judge why it was he was asking that.

"Why do you ask?"

"Every time I've brought her food, she's turned green." The constable shifted uncomfortably. "DCI Stanton thinks that she's pretending, but I'm not convinced."

"He didn't call for a physician?" Thea asked incredulously. Stanton had no way of knowing that Molly was pregnant. For all he knew, she could have gotten ill from the sandwich or the motion of the train. It would have explained why Molly had been in the powder room for so long. If she had fallen ill while talking to Mr. Talbot and had been stuck in there…

"He doesn't think it's necessary. I thought perhaps if I could establish that she was sick before she came in."

"She gets sick when we're on the train sometimes. Not always," Thea lied, "And sometimes food doesn't agree with her. She tries to hide it. I know she's hidden it rather well in the past."

Constable Cooke nodded, believing what she said. "I'll see to it that she gets treated for it then."

"Thank you, Constable. I really appreciate it."

This time the constable gave Thea a real grin before he spoke again. "My lady, I hope you don't mind if I say something a bit forward."

Her brow furrowed. "Go ahead."

"I saw you and Inspector Thayne earlier." Thea nodded, not quite sure where he was going with this. "You are quite a handsome couple, if you don't mind me saying."

Thea blushed, at a loss for words. After all, how did she tell the man that they weren't a couple, that she had never even met Inspector Leslie Thayne before yesterday afternoon?

She glanced away and muttered a quiet "Thank you."

Constable Cooke unlocked Thea's compartment. The horrible bloodspot on the floor quickly soured her mood. It looked worse than she remembered, worse than when the body had been in there, though Mr. Talbot had probably just hidden some of it.

Seeing the aftermath for the second time in two days, Thea was struck again by how obvious it was that there had been a struggle. Mr. Talbot or his killer had grabbed at anything they could reach to try to fight off each other. The hatpin had been evidence that Mr. Talbot had tried to fight back, but Thea hadn't really given it much thought until that moment. He had stabbed his attacker, somewhere, or cut them deep enough to draw blood to coat the metal but hadn't managed to injure them badly enough that the killer hadn't been able to walk away.

"Constable, you know Molly is innocent, don't you?"

He stared at her for a long moment, as if trying to determine if she was questioning him or just stating her belief. After a minute, he gave a curt nod.

"I think Mr. Talbot might have injured his attacker with the hatpin that was found," Thea blurted out. "There was blood on it."

His eyes widened a fraction and Thea bit back a smile. Constable Cooke was much smarter than he acted in front of DCI Stanton. He had caught on immediately to what she was saying.

"I'll have the physician check Molly over for any recent injuries." He paused, as if he was debating his next sentence. "Will you keep an eye out for anyone aboard the train who might have been hurt?"

Thea nodded. "Of course, Constable."

To be honest, she was just happy that he hadn't outright dismissed her idea. Sensing that was as far as the conversation would go, Thea reached up for her case from the rack above her head.

She had kept only two of her smaller cases in her compartment. One held her books and sewing. Her other contained some of her accessories, such as her gloves and jewelry. The attendants had brought it aboard the train and placed it up there and Thea wasn't sure she'd be able to get it down. She had never had to carry them before, let alone try to lift them.

When she made no dent in moving the larger case, she reached for the small jewelry one and pulled it down. It landed against her leg with a thump and she hissed in pain. It might have been smaller, but it was hardly much lighter.

"Can I help you with those, my lady?" Constable Cooke asked. Thea schooled her features, turning to him with the sweetest smile she could muster up.

"That would be very much appreciated, Constable."

He grinned, boyishly. It was a nice smile, she decided. Not

completely unlike Inspector Thayne's. She wasn't sure how someone so sweet could survive under such a cold, callous soul like DCI Stanton, but she was impressed that he had.

The constable reached up, grabbed the valise, and tugged at it. He was clearly struggling but didn't want to come out and say so. He seemed like the kind of man who had been raised to treat women with the utmost respect.

The copy of *A Study in Scarlet* fell to the floor from where it had been tucked on top of Molly's small day bag. Thea frowned as she dipped quickly to grab it from where it landed next to one of the many blood spots. As she descended to the floor, she saw something she had missed before.

At the base of the bench, there was a stain. She didn't notice it before because of the body. It didn't appear as naturally shaped as the rest of the stains. In fact, it looked like someone had drawn letters.

"MSF?" Thea whispered out loud. Clearly Mr. Talbot had tried to leave them a clue as to the identity of his killer.

"Miss Forbes' middle name is Susan. DCI Stanton thinks that perhaps he was trying to write her initials," Constable Cooke said, trying to sound as smart as possible.

But that didn't make any sense. If he was trying to say Molly had killed him, why hadn't he written "Molly," "Mol," or something that would have been obvious? Why write "MSF?" Why had he clung to the hatpin? Mr. Talbot had gone through an awful lot of trouble to try to make his killer known in his last moments.

If Thea had been able to look at the hatpin again, perhaps she could learn something. But she knew she wouldn't get another opportunity to do so. She might have had the chance, had Inspector Thayne not returned to London. She knew better than to think that DCI Stanton would let her return to the police station, let alone see any evidence they had against Molly.

"Perhaps," Thea muttered noncommittally as she stood. She turned and pulled down Molly's beaten and battered day bag from the rack. She held it in front of her body like a shield as she moved away from the compartment and into the corridor.

"Is that all of your things?" the constable asked.

"I do believe so."

Constable Cooke nodded, following Thea into the corridor. He dragged her cases with some difficulty until he cleared the doorframe and could lock the door. He turned to her once more.

"Where did you say you were bringing this, my lady?"

"Compartment C in the next car over." She gave him another saccharine smile and led the way. Constable Cooke huffed, but didn't complain as she led him to the next car and unlocked Wilhelmina's compartment.

He heaved the bags onto the rack that wasn't already occupied by Wilhelmina's suitcase and Thea tucked Molly's tiny valise beside them.

"Is there anything else I can help you with, my lady?" the constable asked, slightly out of breath.

Thea shook her head. "No, thank you." The young man turned to leave, when Thea called out to him again. "Constable?"

He paused, turning back to her with a questioning looking in his eyes.

"Will you look out for Molly?" She trusted this man far more than his superior. She was hoping that he wouldn't allow the man to do anything to her friend.

His brow furrowed, expression softening as he recognized the request for what it was. "Of course, my lady."

"She's innocent," she told him, insistently.

He quirked the corner of his mouth. "I know that, my

lady." His words were surprisingly sincere. He tipped his hat. "Good day."

She smiled in return. "Good day, Constable."

He left the compartment, his footsteps echoing until he left the car.

•

CHAPTER NINETEEN

THE DINING CAR WAS FAR MORE CROWDED THAN THEA WOULD have expected. Extra chairs had been brought in and passengers crowded into the aisles. It was as if everyone in first-class had come to eat at exactly the same moment.

To her surprise, Thea found Wilhelmina sitting with Mr. Poyntz at one of the smaller tables. To her knowledge, they hadn't met before. She paused at the side of the table.

"I hope you don't mind," the American said, "I started without you. I wasn't sure how long you would be held up."

"That's fine." Thea eyed the reporter, who smirked at her in return. "Mr. Poyntz, what a surprise."

"Quite." The man was practically laughing at her. "Do you wish to join us, Lady Theodora?"

Thea stared at him hard for a moment. It was nice to see him with a lighter disposition than he had that morning, but he was far too calculating to have randomly sat with Wilhelmina.

"I take it you two know each other," the American said dryly.

"Lady Theodora was kind enough to grant me an interview yesterday for my paper."

The other woman shot her a curious glance, but Thea shook her head. She didn't want to get into it now. It seemed naïve to have given a newspaperman any information on such events.

"Yes and I would appreciate having a meal without such topics of morbidity," Thea drawled as she sat on the chair a waiter had scrambled to provide.

The reporter chuckled. "Then I'm afraid you're on the wrong train, my lady."

He was right, of course. The tables surrounding them were all glancing at her, discreetly of course. No one would ever risk the social impoliteness of straight out staring at her. There were whispers too. Some passengers at the tables farther away carried on their conversations about her and Molly without a care as to if she could hear it.

It was uncomfortable at best, but she would suffer through it. Thea knew that at the moment Mr. Talbot's murder was the most interesting thing to have occurred. All it would take was the next scandal to hit the gossip cycles and she and Molly would only be old news.

In a way, Thea knew she should be grateful, but she found little comfort in that thought.

"So what shall we talk about?" Mr. Poyntz asked far too innocently for a man in his position as the waiter set lunch before her. The dishes were cramped at the table, but no more than any of the others around them.

"It's lovely weather we're having," Thea said, trying and failing to keep the sarcasm out of her voice.

"I wonder if it might rain?" Wilhelmina added, clearly catching on to what she was saying.

Mr. Poyntz laughed, but continued the conversation with the American woman. Thea was much too distracted to talk. She noticed Nora St. John kept shooting looks towards Thea, though the girl's mother quickly scolded her.

"Are you alright?" Wilhelmina asked concerned.

"Hmm?"

"I think she's referring to the fact that you keep looking at that girl," the reporter inferred helpfully. Thea wanted to glare at him.

"I'm fine," Thea ignored Mr. Poyntz. He seemed unfazed by that fact.

"Does she know you?" Mr. Poyntz asked.

"Not that I know of. I've only seen her aboard the train. I've never actually spoken to her."

The newspaper man seemed a little perturbed by that, though Thea was not sure why he would be. Nora St. John was just a girl. She was hardly likely to be a killer.

Did Mr. Poyntz think the girl was capable of such a feat? Thea didn't want to dwell on that idea for too long. She wanted to avoid that issue, if only just for this meal.

Thea figured that was probably too much to ask for, but she held on to the hope anyway. She was pleasantly surprised that the rest of lunch went on without incident.

"So I've been thinking," Wilhelmina said as the two of them headed into the observation car. "What if whoever wanted Mr. Talbot dead was after the department store? It might not have been the partner. Who's to say he didn't make other enemies?"

The American sat in an empty chair and Thea slipped into the one beside her. The other woman pulled out the papers again.

Thea shook her head. "Or Mr. Fletcher killed him. Molly told me that Fletcher had a gambling problem and according to her, Mr. Talbot had mentioned something about gambling debts and accounting inconsistencies."

Wilhelmina's eyes went wide. "Do you think that Mr. Fletcher was stealing money from Fletcher's to pay for his gambling debts?" She gasped. "That's definitely a motive for murder."

Thea shushed her. In her excitement, the American woman's voice had raised loudly enough for them to get odd looks from the other passengers. The last thing she wanted was for someone else to overhear their conversations. Whoever framed Molly was likely still on the train and might run if they thought that Thea and Wilhelmina were onto them.

They only kept the other passengers' attention for a second until something drew their attention towards the front of the car. Thea stood to see what had drawn the others to look forward and saw a young steward standing awkwardly. He shifted and then moved farther into the car.

"Ladies and gentlemen, if I could have your attention please," the young steward enunciated clearly. He had an excellent speaking voice. "We will be detaching from one of the sleeper cars and then continuing our journey shortly. Again, on behalf of the Great Northern Railway, I apologize for any inconvenience."

Sighs of relief and cheers filled the car. Wilhelmina and Thea shared a glance. Just because the train would be moving again didn't necessarily make it a good thing. When the train reached Scotland, the killer could get off and disappear forever.

At least while it had been stopped in York, Thea had been pretty sure the killer couldn't leave. The train was surrounded by policemen, both uniformed and in plain clothes. No one— save for Thea, Inspector Thayne, and the policemen—had been on or off the train.

The train lurched as the car was disconnected and moved to reconnect to the other cars. As soon as they were connected, the car jerked forward and Thea nearly fell. Steam and smoke billowed up around the outside of the car on the platform as the whole train shuddered forward.

"Perhaps we should move to my compartment," Wilhelmina suggested, rising from the chair with a gracefulness that Thea was envious of. "We can talk more there."

Thea nodded, standing and making sure her footing was solid before she followed the other woman back to her compartment.

ONCE THEA AND WILHELMINA WERE INSIDE WITH THE DOORS closed, she looked around and took a seat beneath the rack with her suitcases.

It was still awkward being in such a small space with a woman Thea had known for less than a day, despite all the time she had just spent with the American.

Something about the whole situation wasn't sitting right with her. Who would have killed Mr. Talbot? He had seemed reasonably pleasant when she had watched him and Molly. He didn't seem like the type to make enemies easily. Though that too could have made enemies. If he had been as nearly a good of man as he had seemed, it could have made someone hate him completely.

"Thank you again for allowing me to stay in your compartment," Thea said.

"That's perfectly fine, darling," Wilhelmina replied, pulling out a shawl to wrap around her shoulders. It had gotten cooler. Thea rubbed at her arms. Despite now having her suit jacket, she found herself wishing that she had Inspector Thayne's coat still. It had been so much warmer. "I know you'd do the same if I was in your place."

Thea wasn't sure that she would. Normally she was content to not get involved in others' affairs. But she didn't want to tell

Wilhelmina otherwise. She wouldn't be the one to disillusion the American woman against her. Thea doubted that she would see the other woman again after this trip.

Thea glanced back out the window.

The train was moving along the track quickly. The wheels were clacking along the tracks. The trees and buildings were passing them by as they traveled. The sun was setting outside the window.

"So I've finished splitting up the list," Wilhelmina spoke again, "I ordered them by importance of people we should speak to."

Thea nodded in agreement. Wilhelmina offered one of the lists and Thea took it. There were a number of names she recognized and a great many more that she didn't.

"I started just with the first-class passengers and the staff. I don't think anyone from the other cars could have gotten to your compartment and left without being noticed."

Thea nodded again. That made sense.

"I also made a list of questions that we probably should ask," Wilhelmina said as she handed Thea a list with a half dozen or so questions.

Thea raised her brow as she read over the list. They were all rather open-ended, allowing the person being questioned to give any number of answers.

Can you tell me what happened before the train was stopped? Where were you during the murder? Who else was with you? Who did you see that looked suspicious? Who did you see in the compartments at the time when Daniel Talbot was killed? Where did you see Molly Forbes at that time?

They were good questions. Wilhelmina had been careful not to include any questions that could be answered with a simple "yes" or "no." Thea wouldn't have thought to ask the questions like that, so she supposed that it was a good thing Wilhelmina was helping her.

Thea looked down at her list. The first name was that of Colonel Bantry. Since he had been with them at the table, she doubted he had seen anything, but he was as good a place as any to start.

Thea stood and straightened her clothes before she tucked the list away into her purse.

"Let's get started. We can meet up around dinner time and see if we've learned anything."

Wilhelmina took her lead and nodded. "That sounds like a plan. You'll come back here to freshen up."

"If that's alright with you."

The American woman waved a hand. "Of course. Now go. The more people we speak to, the better the chance we have of catching the real killer."

Thea smiled slightly at the American's words before she left the compartment.

CHAPTER TWENTY

THEA MOVED THROUGH THE CARS, LOOKING FOR COLONEL Bantry. She found him sitting in the crowded parlor car, reading a newspaper. From the looks of the headlines, it was from the previous day.

There were other passengers around. Some played games. There was a card game going in the front of the car at one of the tables. Other people entertained themselves like the Colonel was, reading newspapers and books and magazines.

She stopped in front of his chair.

"Hello Colonel," Thea greeted him as cheerfully as she could manage. "Do you mind if I join you?"

"Good afternoon, Lady Theodora. Please, sit." He motioned to the empty seat beside him and she took it. "How do you do?"

"I am well. And you?"

"Quite well, thank you."

Thea smiled softly at him. She didn't want the Colonel to be on edge, though she highly doubted he had killed anyone. Not unless his name was actually Forbes and he was really Molly's father.

"I had some questions that I wanted to ask you."

He made a noise of agreement.

"Terrible business, this murder is," he said conversationally, "though I don't have to tell you. I heard it took place in your compartment."

"Yes, but thankfully I wasn't in there at the time. The police are accusing my maid of the murder."

"That's terrible news," the Colonel said sympathetically. "Though are you sure she didn't do it?"

Thea shook her head. "Molly's a sweet girl. I have a hard time believing she could kill anyone, especially in such a fashion," Thea said, thinking back on the gruesome scene. It was pretty much the same line she had been saying to everyone.

"It's quite admirable that you're trying to help your friend," the Colonel said gently, like a father might to his daughter. Thea smiled. She liked him quite a bit. "I'd like to help you however I can. I believe you had some questions?" He prompted.

Thea nodded. "Yes. Where did you go after you left the restaurant car?"

"I went through to the bar to get a drink. I always like a nice glass of scotch after lunch."

Thea nodded, jotting it down in the journal she had rescued from her day bag. It was well-loved, the cover worn from handling it so many times. The pages inside looked like new. Of all the journals she owned, this one was her favorite. Her father had brought it back for her from one of his trips. He had gifted it to her for her birthday the year that he died.

"Did you notice who was in the car with you?"

The Colonel nodded and rambled off some of the names of the people that he knew. Thea checked them off her list and scribbled the names of those he mentioned who weren't on it. She would have to check with them to see if their stories lined up. She would also have to check with Wilhelmina to see if any of the names the Colonel had mentioned were on her list.

"Those were all the people I remember seeing in there," he finished.

"Did you see anything suspicious on your way into the car?"

He shook his head. "No, I'm afraid not. I wasn't paying that much attention." He must have sensed her disappointment because he started speaking again, "I'm sorry I can't be of more help."

Thea shook her head and tried to smile. "That's alright. You have helped." After all, those were a few more people that she could cross off her list.

The Colonel really was a kind man, a proper gentleman. It made no sense that he was still a bachelor. There weren't many men like him anymore. She knew if there had been any at any of the parties she had been to, she would have had made more of an effort.

"Colonel, may I ask you a personal question?"

"Go ahead, my dear."

"Why were you never married?" The Colonel hesitated for a moment and Thea panicked. She had done it again, asked something she shouldn't have. "I'm sorry. I don't know why I asked. You don't have to answer if you feel uncomfortable."

He shook his head patiently. "No, it's fine." He sighed, "There was a woman I loved once when I was a younger man." He frowned, looking off wistfully. "We had a rather whirlwind affair, but in the end, she married another man."

How horrible. Alfred, Lord Tennyson had written that "Tis better to have loved and lost than never to have loved at all." But Thea didn't see how that could possibly be true. If you had never loved in the first place, it would spare you the pain. Like Molly and Colonel Bantry, whose love had only hurt them.

"And so you joined the army," Thea guessed.

"Indeed."

She stayed silent for a few moments, not knowing how she should proceed. She had led the Colonel down this line of questioning.

What Thea didn't understand was how a woman could have passed Colonel Bantry over for some other man? What could the other man have been like? He had to have been pretty spectacular, for a woman to marry him instead of the Colonel. Although, it could have been for money or connections, though the Colonel seemed to have done well for himself.

"So did you keep in touch with the woman?" Thea asked when she finally found her words again.

The Colonel shook his head sadly. "No." He exhaled heavily. "We decided when we parted ways that it'd be for the best. I wrote to her once several years later. She had a happy marriage and children she adored. It was nothing but a youthful dalliance."

He was lying. She could see it in his eyes. He looked too hurt for it to have been nothing.

"You don't believe that. You still love her."

His expression was grim.

Was it better that the Colonel had given up his lady love, or should they have risked being disowned like Molly and Mr. Talbot would have been? Thea imagined that the woman's family wouldn't have been thrilled that she gave up her prospects to marry someone who they didn't approve of.

Of course, that gave Molly's family a perfect motive for murder. They probably blamed Mr. Talbot for taking their daughter away from them, first through marriage and then through her running away to become a maid. They could have killed him in hopes that with Mr. Talbot out of the picture, Molly might come home and maybe even marry a suitor of their choice.

It would have been a cruel fate, if not for Molly and Mr.

Talbot remarrying without either of their parents' knowledge. With Molly owning part of Fletcher's, Mr. Talbot had ensured that Molly would never have to rely on her parents again.

THEA WALKED THROUGH THE REST OF THE PARLOR, questioning everyone she came across. Most of the passengers that she talked to hadn't seen anything. No one really wanted to be involved. Of course, they were more than willing to share any gossip, but the minute they realized she was that Lady Theodora whose maid was arrested, they became silent.

Eventually she worked her way back to the observation car, but the passengers in there were even less helpful.

As if to add insult to injury, every time Thea looked up, Mr. Poyntz was there, scribbling away in his notebook. He followed her to her car, listening in on all of her conversations. She was dying to know what his true motives were, but she had a feeling she might never find out.

With that in mind, Thea glanced at her watch. Upon seeing that it was nearly time for dinner again, she decided that she should head back to Wilhelmina's compartment. The other woman was expecting an update and Thea was hoping that the American had discovered something from the many passengers she had been interviewing.

Thea was in the car when a door that was not Wilhelmina's opened up and a strong pair of arms reached for her. She went to scream, but a calloused, masculine hand covered her mouth. She struggled against him. His grip didn't loosen. She stomped on his foot. He grunted but didn't let go.

"Don't scream," he hissed in her ear. "I'll let you go if you'll be a good girl."

Thea thought about biting his hand in response, but she

wasn't entirely sure what he might do to her. Instead, she nodded meekly, and he let go.

Mr. Poyntz stood in the compartment. His expression was darker than she had seen it in the short time she had known him.

"What do you think you're doing?"

"What?" Thea asked. She didn't even have to pretend she didn't understand his question.

"Playing detectives like that. You need to be more careful. Both you and Mrs. Livingston." His expression was serious. "You're going to get yourselves killed."

"We're fine."

"You've been very obvious with your questions. If the murderer is still on this train, all you've done is likely drawn their attention."

Thea scoffed. "Mrs. Livingston and I have been discreet about this."

Mr. Poyntz laughed. It was cruel and cold and had very little humor in it. "With all due respect, Lady Theodora, you know discretion like a hammer around china."

Thea couldn't help but feel a bit offended by that. She thought they had been doing rather well. It wasn't like the whole train hadn't bore witness to what could have been a relatively private event.

"You need to keep your head down. I don't want you or Mrs. Livingston getting hurt because you stuck your noses in business that the police should have handled."

"Only last night you were being helpful. Now you're telling me to stop. Why?" He stayed painfully silent, avoiding her eyes. It wasn't deliberate. He was trying his hardest to look at a spot just to the right of her face. "You know something."

"I don't."

"Inspector Thayne went to London because he thinks Mr. Fletcher had something to do with killing Mr. Talbot, but you think whoever killed him had nothing to do with Mr. Fletcher and is still on the train," she realized.

"I don't know that." Thea fixed a hard look on him and Mr. Poyntz sighed. "I don't know that for certain," he amended.

Her brow furrowed in confusion. "Then why are you so worried all of a sudden?"

"It's too neat. Miss Forbes gets arrested for killing Mr. Talbot. And now Mr. Fletcher is under suspicion of killing the man." At her surprised look, he shrugged. "You're not nearly as subtle and these doors aren't nearly as thick as you think."

Thea had the good sense to look down sheepishly at that.

"Please be careful. Stop poking around for the moment. Go to dinner. Let me take over for a while and do a little digging."

It went against everything in her to not fight back against that. Thea wanted to tell him that she would be fine, that no one was going to hurt her. But she could see how serious he was, could see it in his eyes that he was terrified for her, so she relented. "Alright."

CHAPTER TWENTY-ONE

THEA RECONVENED WITH WILHELMINA IN HER COMPARTMENT after she left Mr. Poyntz. She wanted to say he was just being paranoid, but everything in her said he was right. They were playing a dangerous game. The killer had to still be on the train and the police were no longer investigating it, so the killer could move freely again. If Thea and Wilhelmina were poking around and found something, it wouldn't be hard for the killer to find out and keep them from talking.

Thea had spoken to most of her list. Several of the passengers had verified each other's stories and whereabouts during lunch and the time after. Wilhelmina seemed equally frustrated. Neither of them were any closer than they had been before. After the hours Thea had spent questioning people, she was exhausted.

"I feel as if I've spoken to everyone on this train!" Thea declared as she entered. She let her shoulders slump as the waves of defeat washed over her.

Most of the people hadn't been truly forthcoming. Some had been downright hostile. Mrs. St. John, the mother of Nora, had been annoyed at her for even asking if she had seen anything. A few people had told her to let the police do the investigating. Mr. Poyntz hadn't been the only one that thought so. More than a few had told her to stop asking questions because the police had already caught the murderer.

"So do I. I've yet to see the Woman in Burgundy," Wilhelmina sighed, and Thea froze. She had almost forgotten about the Woman. She wondered if Mr. Poyntz already knew about her. "I feel like she would have answers, but I didn't see her at all. Did you?"

Thea shook her head. "I haven't seen her since lunch yesterday. But she can't have vanished. No one was allowed on or off the train. Perhaps she's on the second half of the list."

Thea leaned back lightly against the plush leather seat, breathing out. She wanted to be optimistic, but so far, all she had found out was that no one had seen anything. They hadn't made any progress on this. They were no closer to finding the real killer now than they had been hours ago.

"Perhaps," the American woman said softly, relaxing back into her seat as well. She jolted upright suddenly, realizing something. "You got off the train and back on," Wilhelmina pointed out, seeming reenergized.

"But I had a police officer with me. It was hard enough trying to get off with him. I can only imagine if I had tried without him."

To get off the train, Thea and Inspector Thayne had been treated as if they were guilty of something. It was like they were caught trying to break out of prison or rob a bank, like they were criminals. The officers had cross-questioned them before they could get off the train.

Thea straightened back up. "Could the Woman have been in Third Class?"

She doubted it, but she had to ask. The Woman could have snuck back into the first-class cars, into the dining car.

The American seemed much more energized than when

they had reentered the compartment. The new idea had rejuvenated Wilhelmina more than her. Thea couldn't help but feel like they were missing something. They were looking but not observing.

Thea glanced down at her watch. The conductor had announced that dinner would be in less than an hour. The bell had announced the half-hour for dressing before Thea entered the compartment, not that anyone truly had any clothes to change into. Looking up, she noticed that Wilhelmina was doing the same thing, standing up to stretch.

"Perhaps we should wash up for dinner."

Thea nodded. She frowned deeply as a thought occurred to her.

"What's wrong?" Wilhelmina asked.

"My clothes are all in baggage."

"So are mine. So are everyone else's."

But everyone else's clothes weren't in the baggage car. The Woman in Burgundy had changed her clothes. She had a second set of clothes to change into.

Wilhelmina laughed softly. Thea felt a sharp jolt of anger shoot through her. Wilhelmina had been the one to put her on this track to begin with. She had noticed the Woman before but hadn't paid her much attention until the American kept pointing out that they hadn't seen her since lunch yesterday.

Thea breathed in and smoothed her expression into something more neutral and pleasant. The American woman didn't deserve her anger. She had been nothing but kind towards her.

"It's nothing," Thea said, remembering Mr. Poyntz's words, "I'm just going to wash up."

She couldn't get inside the washroom fast enough. She grasped at the sides of the sink, forcing herself to breathe and calm down. It felt like everything was going wrong. She felt trapped, unable to do anything that would actually make a difference.

Thea splashed water on her face and dried it off. It was unfortunate that the water couldn't take away the dark shadows under her eyes. She pulled the pins from her hair, running her fingers through it a few times to get any large knots out. She couldn't do any of the fancy updos that Molly could, but she could put it in a small chignon near the back of her neck. Thea had always found the simple hairstyle to be rather elegant and she figured it would do well enough for dinner.

Thea pinched her cheeks a couple of times to add some color back into them. Looking into the mirror, she saw that she almost looked human again. She forced a smile and went out to rejoin Wilhelmina.

———

"Good evening, Lady Theodora, Mrs. Livingston," the head waiter greeted as they entered the dining car. "May I find the two of you a table?"

"That would be lovely," Wilhelmina declared.

He bowed his head, leading them on to one of the smaller tables. It had been a long time since Thea dined with a friend on a train. Her last close friend, Ilene, married Thea's brother, Cecil. After that, Thea and Ilene had a strained relationship.

The deterioration in their relationship hadn't been by Thea's choice. After all, she had introduced the two and was thrilled for them. It didn't make it any easier to watch them be so happy while she had to deal with their questions of why she was alone still. Not that Ilene hadn't tried to set her up with numerous dull eligible bachelors who were either painfully cocky or afraid of speaking to a woman. She wasn't jealous of them. In fact, Thea was ridiculously pleased that the two of them were so in love, but she missed having Ilene as a friend.

Ever since their daughter had been born, it felt like Thea was farther on the outside than she had ever been.

Dinner passed with good conversation between Thea and Wilhelmina and amiable silences while they ate. By the end of the meal, despite the terrible couple of days she'd had, Thea felt lighter than she had in a long time.

"This has been nice," Thea told the other woman.

The American smiled. "That's a big change from earlier."

Thea grimaced. She didn't mean to be so cold to Wilhelmina when they first met. "You noticed that."

"I'm sure neither of the gentlemen did," she said sweetly. "I'm just good at reading people, and I was deliberately trying to overwhelm everyone."

"Shall we adjourn to the bar car?" the other woman asked brightly.

Thea almost didn't notice that the burgundy clad woman hadn't made an appearance through dinner.

THE LOUNGE WAS QUITE CROWDED AFTER DINNER, THEA realized uncomfortably as she stepped inside. If not for Wilhelmina, she would have turned and darted back out. As it was, she was considering doing just that.

"You need to relax a little," the American woman said softly in Thea's ear. Her breath was against her cheek as she spoke, since it was so loud in the car that she could barely hear herself think.

"I am relaxed," Thea snapped back. In reality, she felt as if she was seconds away from being ill. She hadn't always been so afraid of large crowds, she was sure, but for the life of her, she couldn't remember a time when she didn't feel the tell-tale signs of panic. The thought of a murderer being among them only made the feeling worse.

The lounge was so packed that Thea could hardly move. Instead, she pushed towards a corner seat and watched the crowd. Wilhelmina followed her, watching as Thea tried to make herself as small as possible. This was why she didn't do well at balls and parties, no matter how much she liked looking at the beautiful gowns the women would wear.

Wilhelmina rolled her expressive eyes. "I'll go get you a drink. Stay here."

Thea wanted to laugh. As if she would go anywhere else, not with the way people were bumping into her from every side.

Wilhelmina moved across the car with an elegance that came from being very good around other people. The American was at the bar as she had said, but she was now talking and giggling with a very good-looking man. He said something and she laughed hard, placing her hand on his arm. *It figured that she would make friends so easily*, Thea thought bitterly.

Thea glanced back at the rest of the car. A young woman who had drunk a bit much bumped into her from behind. A young man who was with her chuckled drunkenly. An older woman glared at the two, scolding them. Two older men watched the scene with disapproving eyes.

She glanced back at Wilhelmina. The American woman was already so engaged with her new friend that she wouldn't have noticed if Thea had left. Unable to stand the noise from everyone else any longer, she decided to adjourn to somewhere quieter.

CHAPTER TWENTY-TWO

"Lady Theodora!" Mr. Poyntz's voice came from behind. Thea paused and turned as the man sped his steps to meet her. "Would you like some company?"

The way he asked implied that it wasn't optional. He offered her his arm and she took it. Together, they headed back towards the parlor.

"Have you found anything?" Thea asked.

Mr. Poyntz shook his head. "Nothing yet. It seems like no one knows anything."

They sat down at one of the tables and Mr. Poyntz pulled out his notebook. He flipped through it with near frantic movements.

"How do we know they're even still on the train?" Thea asked him, "How do we know this hasn't all been for nothing?"

Mr. Poyntz ignored her, instead reading through his notebook. Her blood boiled again, as it had when she had spoken to him earlier. She had never before met anyone who enraged her quite so easily.

"Why are you even still helping me?" she asked finally. "What do you get out of this?"

Mr. Poyntz paused and looked up at her. He didn't speak, simply watching her. Just as Thea went to ask him again, he turned his book towards her.

Thea hadn't read through much of the book when she had borrowed it the previous night. She hadn't thought it was necessary.

"Mrs. Fletcher, at King's Cross. Boarded," she read, squinting and turning the book to try to make out Mr. Poyntz's handwriting. It was rather scrawled, like more of his book was. "I'm not sure I understand."

"Mrs. Fletcher is the wife of Lionel Fletcher, Daniel Talbot's business partner." Mr. Poyntz explained. "I saw her boarding this train around the time I was boarding. I met her when I reported on the opening of the department store."

"She's on the train," Thea repeated softly. "Do you think her husband's with her?"

"I don't know," the reporter said, "Perhaps."

"You think Mr. Fletcher murdered Mr. Talbot."

Mr. Poyntz shifted a little, almost uncomfortably as he took his notebook back and tucked it inside his jacket.

"I don't know. But I intend to find out. As for the why I am helping you—" he started to say as the door to the car banged open and Wilhelmina all but fell inside.

The American woman giggled loudly. She had draped herself over the arms of another man. She was swaying dangerously, even as she grasped at his arm. It seemed in the short time Thea had been gone, Wilhelmina had gotten herself well and truly sloshed. She was petting the other man's chest in a way that was most unbecoming for a married woman, or any woman for that matter, to act.

"No, we have to stop," Wilhelmina cried out to the portly, well-dressed gentleman as he tried to pass their table. "Thea, you have to speak with him," she said, interrupting her as she talked to Mr. Poyntz. "He said he saw Molly."

So had a lot of people in the last few days, but Thea didn't want to say that to the woman. Wilhelmina seemed too exhilarated by it and much too drunk to be told otherwise.

The man she had dragged along seemed more of the type to keep to himself, so she was surprised that he would have had come out to tell her about seeing Molly. She was surprised that he was with Wilhelmina as she was acting this way. Still, she wasn't optimistic. No one truly seemed to have seen Molly before she was covered in blood. It colored their opinion of her maid and Thea didn't like it.

Thea turned back to Mr. Poyntz briefly. "Please excuse me," she said, standing up.

The reporter stood as well.

"Of course, Lady Theodora. I'll escort Mrs. Livingston back to her compartment and the two of you can speak here."

Mr. Poyntz offered his arm to Wilhelmina. The woman fell against him drunkenly, so he looped an arm around her waist to keep the American upright. He gently guided her out of the car in the direction of the compartments as he murmured softly to her. The man turned around and looked at her.

"I'm Charles Vaughn. You're Lady Theodora?" he asked. She offered her hand and he shook it.

"Yes. Was Mrs. Livingston right? Did you really see Molly?"

He nodded. "Yes, though I mostly told her so that she would leave without too much of a fuss. I did see the girl, the one they arrested. Her name was Molly?"

Thea nodded and he continued.

"I heard Mrs. Livingston asking the man she was speaking to about Molly. Then I saw someone put something in Mrs. Livingston's drink when her back was turned, but she downed it before I could get to her. I don't know if anyone else saw."

Dread clenched in Thea's stomach. "Did you see who did it?"

He shook his head. "A woman, I believe. I didn't get a clear view. It was crowded in there. I'm sure she was gone by the time I got to the bar though. Lady Theodora, to be frank, I admire the effort you're going through to help your friend," the man said.

"Thank you, Mr. Vaughn. You said that you saw Molly?"

He nodded. "I was heading to the washroom. The one in the next car over was closer than the one in the car I was in. When I left my compartment, I saw Molly, was it, going to leave the washroom. But at the last second, she turned around and went back in. She looked a little green."

Thea figured as much. Molly had told Thea and Inspector Thayne that when they had gone to see her.

"It was another few minutes before the body was discovered, because I was back in my compartment when I heard the scream."

It wasn't a solid alibi for Molly, but it was a far sight better than it had been. After all, it confirmed Molly's story, close enough to mean that the girl had been where she was when she said she was. Thea knew she was, but the police would never find it to be enough to clear her name.

They could say that she had been pretending to be sick. Thea could just hear DCI Stanton now, "She could have gone to the washroom to establish an alibi time, then snuck back to the compartment and killed him, and then returned to the washroom to make sure witnesses saw her coming out."

Though in Thea's opinion, it sounded like an awful lot of work to get caught anyway. How did she know she'd have someone witness her going into the washroom? How could she have known if people would see her on the way out? It left an awful lot to chance and if Molly was nearly as cold-blooded a killer as DCI Stanton swore she was, she would have had a better alibi.

Molly could have changed her mind and joined them in the

dining car or gone into any of the more public cars. If Thea was going to kill someone, that was what she would do. Thea would have killed them and then gone about her business as if nothing was amiss and made certain she had an explanation for where she was. The fact that Molly didn't have an alibi made her seem all the more innocent in Thea's opinion. After all, the killers in books always had solid alibis.

"And you're sure it was Molly you saw heading into the washroom?" Thea asked Mr. Vaughn.

"I'm positive. She looked quite a bit like my niece, same coloring and such. When I first saw her, I thought she was my niece." He chuckled jovially. "I wouldn't have paid attention otherwise. But then I heard Mrs. Livingston asking questions about her."

Thea nodded. It was more than she had before, at least. "Thank you so much for all of your help."

"Not a problem," the man said as they shook hands again. "I do hope Mrs. Livingston makes a swift recovery."

"Thank you," Thea said, bowing her head. The man headed back towards the lounge as she headed towards Wilhelmina's compartment.

CHAPTER TWENTY-THREE

When Thea reached the compartment door, she found it shut. Mr. Poyntz was approaching with a damp cloth in his hand. Thea pushed the door open but didn't go inside.

"Mr. Vaughn thought she might have been drugged," Thea told him, "Do you think that means she was onto something?"

Mr. Poyntz made a frustrated gesture and sighed. "If she's been drugged, when she wakes up, you need to keep her awake." He pursed his lips. "I think it's safe to say that the killer is still on the train."

Thea hesitated. She had known it was a possibility. "Who else would poison her? Wilhelmina and I have been asking questions all afternoon."

Mr. Poyntz offered her the cloth. "I'll see what I can dig up. You should probably put this on Mrs. Livingston's head." He held out his other hand. When she didn't respond, he reached out and dropped a couple of tablets into her hand. Aspirin.

"Thank you."

He gave her a smile. This one was more genuine than the self-confident smirk from before.

"You're welcome, Lady Theodora. Now, please go inside

your compartment and lock the door. I'll feel much better knowing that you both were safe, considering the killer already knows that you're after them."

He waited until she had stepped inside and slid the door shut. Barely a second passed before she yanked the door back open.

"A woman's involved," Thea called after him. Mr. Poyntz pivoted to face her, eyes incredulous. "She might have even been the one to kill Daniel. There was a bloodied woman's boot print outside my compartment door. And Mr. Vaughn saw a woman putting something in Mrs. Livingston's drink."

Mr. Poyntz lifted his head, inhaling sharply.

"That's—" he cut himself off, moving back to her quickly, speaking very quietly, "If this is all related, all by the same person, you should get back into the compartment before I leave and stay there. Do not leave. Do not open the door for anyone except me."

Thea didn't want to understand his panic. Why was he worried for her, a complete stranger? Sure, he had taken care of her... whatever Wilhelmina was to her... acquaintance, friend, stranger, perhaps a little of all of them. They had dined together and had talked, but that didn't make them any more than three strangers who had met under extraordinary circumstances on a train.

Still, Mr. Poyntz waited until Thea was inside her compartment and locked the door before she heard him walk away.

She leaned back against the door, drained from the events of the day. How she was supposed to relax if Mr. Poyntz thought the murderer was after her and Wilhelmina? How was anyone supposed to react to that?

Thea placed the cloth on Wilhelmina's forehead. Wilhelmina had already dozed off. The drug, whatever it had been, had worked quickly for her. Thea was sure that Wilhelmina would have quite the headache when she woke up.

She pulled out the small tray-like table that extended from the wall by the window and placed the aspirin on top of it.

Thea sat down on her bench, curling up as she watched out the window. It was dark outside the window without the lights from the station. It had been such a long day. So much had happened in only two days.

They would be pulling into the station soon and they were no closer to finding the real killer than they had been when they left York. Her mood soured at that thought worse than it already had been.

Thea glanced down at Wilhelmina. If Wilhelmina had just left her alone, she wouldn't be laying there drugged. All because of Thea's need to investigate, of her need to play detective.

If Thea could only find the Woman in Burgundy, perhaps she would finally start getting some answers. The Woman had passed through the sleeper cars at the same time as the killer. If anyone was going to know anything, it had to be that woman. What worried Thea the most was that the Woman seemed to have disappeared into thin air.

Thea jumped as a knock came from the other side of the door. She shook her head. *The killer wouldn't knock on the door*, she told herself. They wouldn't want to alert her.

"Mrs. Livingston? Lady Theodora? I have a telegram for you."

The tension in her shoulders dissolved. It was only a steward.

"One moment," Thea called through the door as she unlocked it, sliding it open a hair.

The steward was one of the younger ones she had seen. He was carrying an envelope in his hands, shifting anxiously.

"My lady," he greeted her, "Telegram just came in for you. From the Scotland Yard," the steward said, offering the message to her. He seemed rather in awe that Thea had someone from Scotland Yard sending her a telegram. She smiled and took it from him.

"Thank you," she said, dismissing him, closing and locking the door before she did anything else.

Thea sat back down before she opened the envelope. Surely enough, it was from Inspector Thayne, but that was all the farther she got before Wilhelmina groaned a little and shifted, pushing herself up a little. The cloth slipped slightly and caught some of her hair.

"My head is wet," Wilhelmina said, squinting up at Thea. "Where are we? What happened? Why is my head wet?"

Thea dropped the note on the seat beside her, standing over Wilhelmina to help her sit up. The cloth fell from her forehead. She groaned again.

"Careful. You were drugged."

"Is that why I'm wet?" Wilhelmina asked, lifting her hand to her forehead. She squinted up at Thea. "I thought I heard someone knocking."

"It was just a steward. I received a telegram."

"Oh," the American said softly, resting her head against the window. Thea imagined the coolness of the window had to feel good against the other woman's head.

"There's some aspirin there if you need them for your head." Wilhelmina shook her head.

"Doesn't hurt," she muttered, her eyes drooping. "Just tired." She yawned, her eyes drooping shut.

Thea patted the woman's cheek, harder than she intended. She felt like she was slapping her to try to keep Wilhelmina awake. Finally, Wilhelmina sat back up properly.

"What?"

"You need to stay awake."

Wilhelmina groaned. "Don't want to. Too tired."

"I know you're tired," Thea said. "But this is important."

"Fine," the woman growled without malice. She yawned and paused mid-way to speak again, "Did you say telegram?"

"Yes, I did."

"What's it say?" Wilhelmina asked. Her eyes drooped shut again as she curled back up on the bench. Thea glared over at her. Wilhelmina let out a pitiful sound and straightened back out again as Thea tore open the envelope.

"It's from Inspector Thayne," she told her as she skimmed the paper. "It says that they arrested Lionel Fletcher on suspicion of murder. He had gambling debts. He had a train ticket from York yesterday."

But that didn't make any sense to Thea. How would Lionel have gotten off the train at York? How did he know he'd be able to get off the train and return to London before anyone came looking for him? How could he have been on the train and no one had seen him?

Not only that, if he was the killer and was no longer on the train, then who had drugged Wilhelmina?

Thea read on. "They're releasing Molly in York. She's taking the next train to Scotland."

"Good then," the other woman smiled sleepily. "Can sleep now."

Wilhelmina laid her head down before Thea could stop her. She jumped from her bench, grabbing Wilhelmina's shoulders and shaking her. She wouldn't wake up, so Thea slapped her, harder this time. She left a little bit of a red mark on the other woman's face, but at least she was awake.

"What's that for?" she slurred, eyes cracking open a fraction.

"You can't go to sleep," Thea ordered.

"But—"

"Wilhelmina, if Lionel Fletcher is the killer and they arrested him in London tonight, who drugged you?"

Her bleary eyes blinked up at her completely confused. "I don't know."

Thea felt unsatisfied with the answer that Lionel Fletcher had killed someone. Something still wasn't right. Should she feel better, knowing the real killer was behind bars? If it was true, shouldn't she feel better instead of that overwhelming sense of dread?

"This doesn't feel right," Thea complained.

"Be happy. Molly's free."

"But who drugged you?" Thea demanded and the American shifted upwards slightly. "Mr. Vaughn saw a woman drug your drink."

"Woman?" Wilhelmina asked again and Thea sighed frustrated, turning towards the window. "What about the Woman?"

The Woman? Wilhelmina wasn't making any sense. Thea had just told her that a woman had drugged her.

"Burgundy," Wilhelmina slurred again.

It took her a second to translate that into her mind.

The Woman... burgundy. Wilhelmina had called the Woman from the restaurant car that before. The Woman in Burgundy.

Thea put a hand over her mouth at the realization. The Woman in Burgundy was still missing.

The pieces all clicked in her head. That woman was somehow the key to all of this.

CHAPTER TWENTY-FOUR

"Lady Theodora?" the young woman's voice came out shaky. Nora looked quite apprehensive. She kept looking down the corridor like she was worried someone might see her. "I beg your pardon. I wasn't able to get away from my mother before." She shifted in her spot. "May I come in?"

Thea nodded, moving her arm to let the girl inside. She darted inside and closed the door behind her, locking it. She seemed quite panicked.

Thea's brow furrowed. She wasn't sure why the girl was here or what she might have wanted. It seemed strange to entertain the notion that this young girl could be the killer.

"My name is Nora St. John. My mother and I are traveling together," she introduced herself, unaware that Thea already knew exactly who she was.

Nora sat down on the bench next to Wilhelmina, glancing at her worriedly.

"I—" she started, eyeing the woman beside her. Wilhelmina straightened up, looking rather put off that she couldn't sleep. Nora swallowed and started again. "I- I heard that you were investigating the murder. I saw something, before and then just a little while ago in the bar car." She glanced at Wilhelmina again. When she spoke, her voice was hysterical. "I saw a woman leaving your compartment, but I don't think she saw me. I'm certain she didn't see me. I hid before she saw me. I saw the same woman near her earlier." She motioned to Wilhelmina.

Thea swallowed hard. That was promising but also nerve-racking. It confirmed everything that Thea thought she knew.

"This woman, she wasn't Molly?" she asked once more because she had to be sure. There was no way Molly could have poisoned Wilhelmina's drink, but she did still have the opportunity to have killed Mr. Talbot, no matter how unlikely that was.

It was a relief when Nora shook her head.

"I don't think so. I had a good view of her when I was waiting to be questioned by DCI Stanton. I told him about the Woman, but he just assumed it was Molly. But it wasn't. She was wearing a burgundy suit and hat. I watched her take off her boots in the hallway once she left the compartment. I thought it was quite peculiar that she would do such a thing."

Thea inhaled sharply.

"She took her boots off?" That explained why the tracks didn't go very far. Perhaps the Woman had seen that she had blood on her and didn't want to leave a trail.

Nora nodded. "And then she headed in the other direction. I don't know where she went, but it was towards the back of the train."

Towards the back of the train, Thea thought. The Woman in Burgundy must have had a compartment in first-class.

Thea breathed in, heart racing at the thought. The police had most certainly arrested another innocent man. The Woman had tried to kill Wilhelmina. She didn't care about just killing Mr. Talbot or about letting Molly or Lionel Fletcher hang. Perhaps she wasn't working with Mr. Fletcher.

If she was, wouldn't she have cared that the man had been arrested?

She was more ruthless than Mr. Poyntz even knew.

Mr. Talbot had told them that the Woman had the initials MSF when he wrote them in his own blood. Thea was willing to bet that Mrs. Fletcher's initials were MSF. Mr. Talbot would have known her. It made sense that he would have tried to tell them if she had been the one to do that.

But what reason would that woman have to get rid of her husband, assuming that Mrs. Fletcher and the Woman in Burgundy were the same person? Perhaps she thought owner-ship of the company would revert to her husband after his partner's death? Maybe Mrs. Fletcher had never intentionally framed him or she might have thought that by doing so, she would gain control of the company. It was a far better motive than Molly's.

"Did you go to look after she left?"

Nora shook her head. "No. I didn't think too much of it. I thought it might have been her compartment, but I remem-bered it because it was odd that she was removing her boots. It wasn't until after the body was found that I ever made the connection." The girl frowned deeply. "I wish I had gone to look now. Perhaps that poor girl wouldn't have been arrested if I had. And she might be—" she cut off, glancing at Wilhelmina with a sob.

"There, there," Thea said, kinder than she normally would have as she patted the girl's shoulder awkwardly. "It's not your fault." After all, she had brought her a new lead and clear evidence that Molly had not killed Mr. Talbot. Just because Molly was cleared didn't mean she was comfortable with the idea of allowing an innocent man to hang for Mr. Talbot's murder. She was feeling rather generous.

The girl smiled at her, but it wasn't very reassuring. Her eyes were watery and she was terrified.

"Out of curiosity, why didn't you say anything before?"

"Because of my mother." Nora shifted uncomfortably. "She's the one who's been taking people's things." The girl glanced down, unable to meet Thea's eyes for very long. "She just can't help herself. She sees things and she has to have them. I try to put them back when I can, but I didn't want to get caught."

"So your mother's the thief that Mrs. Beauvale has been raving about?"

Nora grimaced. "Unfortunately, yes." She held out her hand, revealing the ugliest emerald brooch Thea had ever seen. It explained why fashion-conscious Wilhelmina didn't want to wear it out of her compartment in the first place.

"Is that Mrs. Livingston's?"

Nora nodded, cheek coloring.

"I'm terribly sorry for the trouble my mother caused." Thea gave her what she hoped was a reassuring smile and the girl continued, "I don't know what to do."

"Can you stay here for now? Keep her, Mrs. Livingston," Thea clarified, "awake. Lock the door once I leave."

"What?" Nora asked as she jumped from the seat. "Where are you going?"

"To talk to the conductor. If I'm not back before the train reaches Edinburgh, call the police and Inspector Thayne at Scotland Yard."

"But—"

Thea shushed her.

"It'll be fine. Just don't open the door for anyone but me or a reporter named James Poyntz."

Nora nodded and followed Thea over to the door. Thea swept from the room and the door slid shut behind her.

CHAPTER TWENTY-FIVE

IT WAS WITH DETERMINED FOOTSTEPS THAT THEA HUNTED down the conductor. He was doing his best to make sure things were running smoothly, especially after all the excitement of the day. She had a feeling it was about to get much more exciting though, at least for her.

It might be a long shot, but it was better than any chance they'd had before.

"Excuse me," she said to him as she found him. "I was wondering about another passenger."

"What were you wondering, my lady?"

"A female first-class passenger, Mrs. Fletcher. She's been wearing a red suit and then a dress." She gave him her most charming smile. "Do you happen to remember what compartment she's in?"

He thought for a moment, staring quietly and blankly ahead. "Of course. She's in Compartment E in the last sleeper, the one just before the parlor."

Thea nodded. "Thank you so much for your help."

He bowed his head. "Of course, my lady. Anytime."

———

THEA MOVED CAREFULLY THOUGH THE SLEEPER CARS, WATCHING each door warily for Mrs. Fletcher. Several passengers exited and gave her odd looks, but all moved out of her way.

When Thea finally reached Mrs. Fletcher's car, she slowed. Her steps became measured, trying not to make a sound. The last thing she wanted to do was alert the Woman that she was onto her. Especially not after Mrs. Fletcher had proven herself willing to do whatever it took for them not to find her.

The door to Compartment E slid open as Thea came up to it and the Woman in Burgundy stepped out. Her limp was more pronounced now. She began to walk towards the wash-rooms, until she caught sight of Thea and froze.

"Excuse me," Thea said, approaching the woman carefully, like she was coming up to a wounded animal ready to attack. She would pretend like she had no idea who this woman was or what she had done. "My name is Lady Theodora Prescott-Pryce. I saw you yesterday in the dining car. You were passing through the sleeper car during lunchtime."

Thea didn't want to tell Mrs. Fletcher that she knew the other woman had been in her compartment. That sounded too accusing, too hostile. She didn't want to put the Woman on guard.

A look of panic flashed over Mrs. Fletcher's features. It passed so quickly that Thea almost missed it, but it seemed Mrs. Fletcher knew exactly what Thea was talking about.

"What of it?" Mrs. Fletcher said coldly, with no trace of the momentary apprehension that had been on her face before.

"I was just wondering if you had seen anything as you passed through," she replied softly, though she asked it more as a question. In her mind, she finished the sentence with 'Did you happened to stick a knife into Daniel Talbot's chest when you went into my compartment?'

The Woman stuck her nose up in the air, playing up a haughty air. "I saw nothing."

Knowing she was fighting a losing battle, Thea went to apologize for bothering her, to thank Mrs. Fletcher for her time when she saw it. A glint of garnet caught her eye from on top of the Woman's head. It was the hairpin that matched the one that Mr. Talbot had been holding, the one he had grabbed off of his killer.

Thea swallowed slightly. The Woman in Burgundy hadn't just been a witness as Wilhelmina had suspected. No, instead Thea had been right. Mrs. Fletcher was the real killer. She had murdered Mr. Talbot in cold blood. She had framed Molly and then her husband. Not that Thea hadn't guessed, but this was the confirmation she wanted.

"You did it," Thea stupidly muttered under her breath in shock. It was not so much about the realization, but that the Woman was so foolish as to blatantly flaunt that she killed the man, "You killed him."

The Woman's face turned hard. She swung her purse as hard as she could, knocking the breath out of Thea's chest. The Woman took advantage of Thea being doubled over and she turned and ran down the corridor as fast as she could.

Thea coughed, struggling to regain her breath. Her corset had taken the brunt of the blow, but she was still left quite winded and it had hurt.

"Lady Theodora?" Mr. Poyntz asked as the Woman ran past him. Thea hiked her skirts up to her knees and ran after her.

"The Woman in Burgundy," she called back, "She's the killer!"

Thea pulled the door open and crossed to the next car. The Woman was still running, just barely ahead of her. It seemed that the limp was from a recent injury, perhaps the one that Mr. Talbot himself had inflicted with the hatpin.

They dodged the other passengers and stewards as the two women raced between cars, farther into the train.

They ran until there was no train left. As the Woman turned towards her, Thea saw the caged-panicked look in her eyes.

The Woman glanced back and forth between Thea and the railing that surrounded the end of the train. She was going to jump, Thea realized with no small amount of dread.

The Woman's face darkened and she reached up to her hat, extracting the second of the garnet hatpins and aimed it like she was wielding a sabre.

She could either jump or kill Thea. The question was which would the Woman chose?

Thea inhaled sharply. She should have expected this.

The Woman circled her, until Thea was facing the entrance back into the observation car, her back was to the tracks behind them. Thea stepped back, trying to place more distance between them. She did that until she realized her back was against the railing. She wanted to wince from her own stupidity.

Thea swallowed, gathering an amount of courage she didn't think she had. She studied the Woman. Mrs. Fletcher was supposed to be a cold-blooded killer, yet her hands were shaking as she held the pin. So cold and calculating, yes, but she certainly wasn't up to killing someone spontaneously. She must have planned for a long time before she killed Mr. Talbot.

"If you're going to kill me, then will you first tell me why you did it?" The Woman was silent. "Why did you kill Mr. Talbot?"

"He had it coming to him," she spat, "The scum. He refused to give Mr. Fletcher the money he was due. He did all the work and Mr. Talbot just reaped the rewards of my husband's actions."

"So you killed him."

"I'd kill him a thousand times!" She screamed. "Him and his whore. They didn't earn any of this!"

Thea shook her head. "They deserved a lot better than what you did to them." The Woman stepped closer. "Why did you frame your husband by killing Mr. Talbot?"

Mrs. Fletcher scoffed. "Lionel brought this upon himself. He's always been such a wimp, pathetic. If he had just stood up to that filth, I wouldn't have had to do anything to Mr. Talbot and I certainly wouldn't have needed to let Lionel take the fall." She shrugged. "Now my hands are clean of the lot of them."

Thea stared incredulously. Had this woman honestly killed Mr. Talbot because she thought her husband should ask for more money to pay for his gambling? It seemed so stupid. Why would she even think that killing him would make her problems disappear?

It was strange how unrepentant someone could be with such fragile logic. The Woman was clearly insane. The fact that she thought that anyone deserved what she had done to them proved that she was mad. Thea wouldn't have wished what Mrs. Fletcher had done on her worst enemy, let alone her friends.

"And Mrs. Livingston? Why did you poison her?" she asked.

"That slut had been asking around about me. She was so close to figuring everything out. I knew you had been asking around too, but you're so out of your league, little girl."

Honestly, she found that insulting. She had figured that this Woman was involved, had even toyed with the idea of her being involved, long before she had Wilhelmina's help. It was just a shame that Wilhelmina had been so obvious about her suspicions.

How she thought she could get away with it was beyond her. But she had almost done just that. The police had been content to let her do so, despite all the evidence that pointed towards her. It was sickening.

Which led her to her next question.

"Did you have help from the police to frame Molly? No one with half a brain would think she could have actually done it."

The Woman scoffed again. "Anyone can kill anyone, if properly motivated. It just turns out that Margaret Forbes had plenty of motive."

That wasn't an answer.

The Woman took a step forward. Thea leaned back, trying to get as far as she could away from the pin. The Woman dove at her and Thea ducked away, grabbing onto the rail tightly as she slid closer to the edge. The train's jostling wasn't helping. Any small slip could kill her. And Mrs. Fletcher's pin was just as dangerous. Neither would be a very pleasant way to die.

She gripped the railing tighter as they hit another bump in the tracks. Mrs. Fletcher had stopped moving forward. Thea thanked her lucky stars that the Woman seemed content to just stand there, waiting for Thea to move, to slip. The way the train kept bouncing them, that might not be long.

Thea felt as if her heart might race from her chest, she could hardly hear the wind gusting around her, the pounding in her ears was so loud.

Thea was going to die, she knew. She was going to die and Mrs. Fletcher would get away with everything. She obviously had someone helping her, a policeman or someone on the inside, keeping her from jail. They would get away with it too.

It didn't seem fair to poor Lionel Fletcher that he had been married to a woman who was so willing to frame him for murder. He would hang. All because Thea had messed up so terribly as to go after Mr. Talbot's killer with no help.

Where was Mr. Poyntz? He had been right behind her. Thea had passed him in the corridor and he knew she had been chasing Mr. Talbot's killer. Why wouldn't he have followed them?

Thea struggled to keep her footing and her fingers were slipping and it was only getting worse. She struggled to hold on to the railing tighter as the train jostled around slightly.

A rush of footsteps came closer. The sound stopped short as they realized what was happening. The person didn't want to get too close, that much was clear. They must have thought that Mrs. Fletcher might notice and might kill Thea, no hesitation. She had to keep the other woman's attention on her.

"What happened? Why kill him now?" Thea asked Mrs. Fletcher. She wanted to keep the Woman talking, wanted to keep her eyes away from whoever might burst through the door.

"That horrible man deserved to die!" she screamed. "Talbot was trying to cut my husband out of the business. My husband said that Talbot had put a clause in about his gambling, but it only made him gamble more." Mrs. Fletcher pressed her fingers to the spot between her nose and her eyes. "I couldn't stand it anymore. It was Mr. Talbot's fault that Mr. Fletcher started gambling in the first place. If that wicked man hadn't been so selfish with the profits, Mr. Fletcher wouldn't have needed to supplement his income."

"Step away from her, miss!" the conductor's voice came clearly over the squealing and grinding of the wheels. Mrs. Fletcher turned as the train lurched forward. As she saw the conductor, the Woman stuck her hatpin to Thea's throat like a knife.

"Stay back!" the Woman screamed over the noise. "Or she's dead too."

"Mrs. Fletcher," Thea cried out, feeling the cold metal of the pin brush her neck. She wanted to kick herself. Inspector Thayne and Mr. Poyntz had warned her. They had told her not to get involved, to stay in the compartment. She just

couldn't have listened? "This is just between you and me." She
darted her eyes towards the conductor. "Go, now!"

"No!" the Woman shouted. "He's a part of this now too.
He knows. He's seen my face. He can't go anywhere."

Thea didn't think it was a good time to point out all the
faces pressed to the windows of the observation car, watching
the three of them like it was the most exciting show they had
ever seen. Perhaps it was the most exciting thing they had ever
seen. Most people lived such dull lives. Her grandmother
would have a fit if she ever heard about this.

The least of Mrs. Fletcher's worries should have been if the
Conductor had seen her face. The entire train stood witness to
her confession. She had confessed to everything, framing
Molly, framing her husband.

The only thing Thea didn't know was the name of the
policeman or policemen who helped her frame Molly initially.
Thea glanced at the Woman, studying her features in profile as
she glanced nervously between Thea and the Conductor. It
wasn't exactly as if Thea could go anywhere. If she were to
move, the hatpin would pierce her throat. If she were to fall,
she would land on the tracks. At the speed they were going, she
probably wouldn't die instantly. She would suffer a slow,
lingering death.

Thea had a hunch though, that if she could get it out
before either thing happened, perhaps it would tell them who
the corrupt policeman was.

"Mrs. Fletcher, what does the 'S' in your name stand for?"

"What?" the Woman asked incredulously, thrown off by
such seemingly out of the blue question.

"Your initials are MSF, right?"

"Yes," Mrs. Fletcher said slowly, as if she couldn't figure
out where she was going with this. Which was good. Thea
didn't want her to know. If she did, she might not tell her.

"So what does the 'S' stand for?"

Mrs. Fletcher stared at her, looking as if she was trying to figure out what Thea could possibly get by telling her.

"Stanton," she said slowly.

"MSF," Thea whispered under her breath again. She was the person Mr. Talbot was trying to tell the police killed him. They just hadn't listened. They hadn't been willing to listen.

The name Stanton explained so much. Had they planned it together then? Had they planned for Mrs. Fletcher to get on the train, to kill Mr. Talbot, and then to ride the train until the end, undetected? Had they planned for DCI Stanton to take over the case? Had Molly just been convenient then? It seemed, the way she kept talking, that she had intended to frame her husband all along, that Molly had just been happy collateral damage. Thea doubted that either Mrs. Fletcher or DCI Stanton expected Mr. Talbot to implicate his own wife.

Something moved behind the conductor in the shadows. It moved closer and a flash of something shiny caught the light.

Carefully, Thea brought her hand up while the Woman was distracted. She wanted to get the hatpin before it could pierce her throat by accident. The adrenaline raced through her veins. Mrs. Fletcher was going to kill her, Thea just knew it. The worst part was that it would be a complete accident. That perhaps scared her more than the thought of dying, that her death would be an accident, right here, right now.

The shot went off before Thea knew what had happened. The hatpin slipped in the Woman's hand, barely nicking her throat before Thea could stop it completely. Thea cried out in relief as she dropped the pin to the ground. The Woman kicked her feet out from under her as she collapsed and Thea grasped tightly to the railing. Mrs. Fletcher was on the ground, clinging to her right shoulder.

James Poyntz stood with a revolver smoking in his hands. He was steady, despite the jolting movement of the train. His expression was hard, cold, emotionless. He lowered the weapon as he came closer, keeping it trained on Mrs. Fletcher.

"Move away from the edge," Mr. Poyntz ordered the Woman. Mrs. Fletcher crawled slightly over before he pointed the revolver again. "Don't move." The Woman swallowed and did as he said. "Help Lady Theodora," he called to the conductor, who was standing helplessly as she tried to get a better hold on the edge of the speeding car. She felt as if she was getting dangerously close to the tracks.

The conductor reached out for her hand, but Thea couldn't grab it without letting go of the train. The car was jerking too much for her to let go.

Colonel Bantry had pushed his way out onto the platform and moved past the indecisive conductor. He reached out to Thea and grabbed her around the waist, pulling her back so she was safely aboard the train.

"Let's get you inside, Lady Theodora," the Colonel said as he led her into the observation car. She moved with a steadiness that no one who had just been through an ordeal should have had. Her legs moved fine. Perhaps it would just take a while before it hit her.

CHAPTER TWENTY-SIX

"Move aside," the Colonel called to the crowd that had gathered at the door. Colonel Bantry's military bearing must have scared some of their viewers, because they did as he said and moved. "Is there a doctor anywhere?" he called out as he gently guided her to a chair.

A steward was moving forward, pushing through the spectators as he led a man with a case. "I've got one here."

"What happened?"

"That woman attacked her with a hatpin."

Time felt like it was moving strangely as the doctor looked at her neck, cleaning it with something that burned a lot. Thea felt the train pull into the station, saw the police meeting them there. No one was allowed off the train again. She bit her lip, trying not to cry out as the cleaner stung. He put something cold on it and then a bandage.

"You'll be fine. It's actually not deep at all. Just a scratch. You were very lucky. People have been killed with hatpins before."

The doctor didn't realize the irony of his statement.

The doctor stood and turned to the Colonel. "She's mostly

just had a shock. Someone should probably stay with her. I can give her a mild sedative."

"No," she protested, "No medicine."

The doctor looked to the Colonel, like she wasn't capable of making her own decisions. Perhaps he thought the Colonel was her father.

"That won't be necessary. Thank you, Doctor," Colonel Bantry said to the man, shaking his hand.

"Wait," Thea cried out hoarsely, "Wilhelmina."

The two men turned to stare at her like she was crazy.

"Lady Theodora," the Colonel said gently. "Mrs. Livingston hasn't been seen since she was in the lounge."

"She was drugged," she choked out. She was having a hard time speaking. Her mind told her it was psychological. "Mrs. Fletcher drugged her." She wiped at her eyes with her hand. Colonel Bantry offered his handkerchief to her and she took it gratefully and dabbed at her eyes with the soft cloth. "She's in her compartment."

The Doctor nodded. The steward stepped forward. "I can show you the way, sir."

"Thank you." They both left, moving through the crowd that parted like it was the Red Sea.

Thea thought about standing, but that didn't really seem like it was something she'd be able to do right now. Her legs and arms had turned to mush from holding on so tightly to keep her grip standing and her throat hurt like she had been screaming. The ringing in her ears got louder the longer she sat there. The worst part was she never felt more alive.

Mr. Poyntz walked into the lounge some time later. James, she thought, because really if he was going to shoot another person for her, Thea figured that probably put him on a first-name basis, at least in the privacy of her own mind.

The police had arrested Mildred Stanton Fletcher and

taken her away, though the uniformed men were still dealing with the tribal matters that followed such an affair.

Thea let her head fall down. There were too many people staring, their eyes all on her. As she looked into her lap, she could see why. Her clothes had spots of blood, probably from Mrs. Fletcher.

James stepped up to her and seeing what she was looking at, he pulled off his jacket and wrapped it around her. The jacket was rather warm. She hadn't realized just how much she had been shivering until he did so. He crouched before her like she was a child.

"Are you alright, Lady Theodora?"

No! Thea wanted to scream out. Did she look like she was alright? Did she look like she'd ever be alright again? She was some sort of freak, who liked being in danger. Because the truth was that she had never felt more alive than she had hanging off the back of the train, Mrs. Mildred Stanton Fletcher holding the pin to her throat. It made her sick to think of how perfectly fine she felt.

"I'm okay," she said instead. "All thanks to you."

The corners of his lips quirked up. "No, it's not. You're a fighter, Theodora Prescott-Pryce. You would have been just fine without me."

Somehow, deep inside, Thea knew his words to be true. Somehow, she would have figured a way to keep Mrs. Mildred Stanton Fletcher from killing her. Which reminded her...

"Did anybody notify the Leeds City Police?" she asked. "DCI Stanton is corrupt. He's the one that framed Molly, all because he didn't want his relative to take the blame for it."

James' expression hardened and he stood up. "No, but I'll do that right now."

"Mrs. Fletcher had been trying to frame her husband, but he had nothing to do with Mr. Talbot's death. Could you tell Inspector Thayne that?"

"Of course, my lady."

"Before you go," Thea began, because she needed to know. She would always wonder about it if she didn't. "Where did you get the gun?"

"From Colonel Bantry, of course," and she knew he was telling the truth. "I saw it in his compartment earlier when I went for a statement about everything that had happened today."

Lie.

Thea didn't know how he was lying, but she was positive he was. She was sure that the gun had come from Colonel Bantry, but James hadn't seen it in the Colonel's compartment. She didn't believe it was James' gun. He fought his wars with words, though he was clearly not averse to weapons. He couldn't be, considering how comfortable he had been shooting Mrs. Fletcher.

"Why?" James asked. Such a simple, loaded word. It held so many questions.

Thea shook her head, trying to play it off like she was still in shock over everything that had happened. "I was just curious."

There was so much more to James Poyntz than what met the eye. He was an enigma, and she wanted to know why he kept seeking her out. He wasn't just the pushy journalist he had first appeared to be. Nobody on this train seemed to be who they presented themselves as. Thea was beginning to think that she was not even the same woman she had been when she first boarded the train.

James chuckled. "Don't you know what they say about curiosity?" he asked again, clearly buying her confusion. Thea giggled when she realized he was joking. Because any normal person would do so at a joke. "The police will be here shortly to interview you," he told her. "They're just working their way through some of the other witnesses to give you a chance to recover."

"I appreciate that," she said, and found that she really did. After all, they could have been more like DCI Stanton, insisting on making her as uncomfortable as possible. Instead, they were waiting for her to recover, like any other normal woman.

But Thea was more upset by how not upset she was. She didn't feel any of the nervousness inside that she had before. She felt all sorts of upside down at the thought that she felt perfectly fine. Any other person would have been upset at the situation, not upset that they weren't more afraid.

Thea looked up at James as he stood up. "Do you want me to stay?"

She shook her head. "I'll be okay. Would you check on Wilhelmina? Mrs. Livingston," she said, seeing his confusion. "Tell me how she is?"

He nodded. "Of course."

James said something to one of the stewards as he left the car, passing through the crowd of people who she seemed fated to be around on this trip. The steward disappeared as James left the car and returned several moments later with a glass of water and a glass of something amber in color, which she assumed to be liquor. He placed them on the table beside her.

Thea assumed James had sent it over to her. Her nerves were shot. She took the glass of brandy and tipped her head back, downing a sip without hesitation. She cradled the glass between her hands. The water looked too cold for her taste at the moment, its condensation beading down onto the table below.

Thea hated the looks of pity people kept giving her. The other passengers watched her as they waited for their turn to be questioned about what had happened. It was putting her on edge.

The police from Edinburgh finally arrived. The one who came to her was not nearly as young as Inspector Thayne, nor as cruel as DCI Stanton. He had kind eyes and was graying at the temples but didn't really show his age.

"I'm Inspector Reid. I hear we have you to thank for catching a killer and a corrupt copper, my lady."

She inclined her head in acknowledgment as the inspector sat down across from her.

"How did you manage to figure out that Stanton was the one who framed Mrs. Talbot when the rest of the department didn't? They worked with him all the time. They should have known."

Thea shrugged. "They were too close to him. He refused to look beyond Molly. I knew something wasn't right."

The man smiled. "If you had been a man, you might have made a great detective."

Thea could feel her smile dimming a little but decided she would take it as a compliment. She refused to be offended by the idea that if she had just been born a man, she would have had fewer problems in life. After all, they did live in a man's world.

"I'll take that in the spirit in which it was intended."

Inspector Reid flushed slightly. It was strange to see a man nearly Colonel Bantry's age doing so. "Right. I apologize. That was rude."

She wasn't going to say that no it wasn't, because it was a little. But he hadn't meant it.

"I mean no offense," Inspector Reid continued, stumbling through. "Could you tell me what happened?"

She did just that, starting from the beginning, when she first noticed Mrs. Fletcher at lunch to when she had found Mr. Talbot's body on the floor. She told the inspector about the police arresting Molly, about knowing something still wasn't right, about Mrs. Livingston's poisoning. She told him how

Nora had spotted Mrs. Fletcher as she was leaving Thea's compartment and continued until he knew about everything.

"I appreciate your help in all of this, Lady Theodora," he said formally.

Inspector Reid stood up and shook her hand. James was waiting for her at the other end of the car when she finally stood up and moved down there. He seemed very comfortable there, watching the few that remained in the car.

"Mrs. Livingston will make a full recovery, the Doctor says," he informed her. "She'll just need to sleep it off. Mr. Vaughn stopped her from drinking too much of it and saved her."

"I'm glad," Thea said, finding that she meant it.

"Are you sure you're alright?" he asked again, glancing up and down at her. It was like he was expecting something that wouldn't be there, something that should have been there and wasn't.

"Can I escort you back to your compartment?"

Thea nodded, taking James' arm as he offered it. They made their way through the bustling cars, pushing past until they reached Wilhelmina's compartment.

CHAPTER TWENTY-SEVEN

Nora St. John had remained in the compartment, despite wanting to return to her mother. Inspector Reid was interviewing her about Mrs. Stanton and her mother's thieving. Wilhelmina was sitting up now that the doctor had cleared her.

"I think that covers everything," the inspector said as he stood up. He bowed his head before he moved from the room. "Ladies, gentleman."

Inspector Reid disappeared around the corner and James helped her grab her luggage down from the rack. She appreciated his help, especially as he did the same for Wilhelmina.

"I should probably get back to my mother," Nora said to them. "She's got to be worried sick."

Somehow, Thea highly doubted that, but she refused to argue with the girl. Instead, she reached out to the girl, clasping her hands warmly. "Thank you for all your help, Nora."

The girl shook her head, her cheeks turning red from the attention. "I didn't do much at all."

"You did a lot more than you know," Wilhelmina said sleepily. The girl blushed deeper and left. Wilhelmina rubbed her eyes. "I'll probably get a room here tonight. I don't want to travel anywhere more tonight."

"That sounds like a good idea," Thea admitted, "I'm sure my cousins probably already have. They're both rather practical."

Wilhelmina smiled.

"Then, perhaps I will see both of you in the morning before we all leave. I do believe I'll be staying in Edinburgh tonight as well." James bowed his head to both of them. "Goodnight."

The reporter moved through the compartment doors and disappeared down the corridor. Thea smiled at the other woman.

"I suppose it's time for us to get off the train," Wilhelmina said.

"I agree," Thea said, reaching for her small case and Molly's bag. It didn't look like it belonged to a middle-class girl. It didn't fit with what she now knew about Molly at all. "I'm sorry for involving you in all of this," she told the American.

Wilhelmina shook her head. "Don't apologize. I involved myself in this, not you. And I don't regret doing so for a moment."

Thea smiled back at her, gripping Wilhelmina's hands tightly. Wilhelmina made her feel much warmer inside, more normal. She wondered if they could stay on the train, to not get up. She was feeling very tired all of a sudden, as if all her strength had disappeared after everything that had happened.

With the last bit of energy in her body, Thea pushed herself up and walked out the door.

———

ANTHONY AND CHARLOTTE WERE WAITING ON THE PLATFORM for her when Thea climbed off the train. Inspector Reid informed her that Molly would be coming in on the morning train and Thea wanted to be there for her.

Charlie looked like she might scream when she saw her. Her eyes grew wide as she saw the blood on her cousin's clothes. Thea tried to shush her before the whole station could hear and pulled James' jacket tighter around her. She didn't want to cause more of a scene than there already had been. She should have changed before she left the train, but she didn't have any clothes to change into.

"How are you doing?" Anthony asked, looking her over carefully. He must have been satisfied with what he saw, because he didn't push too much. Thea hated how he was acting, like she was fragile and might break down at a moment's notice. She felt much too worn out to do so though. She had cried all of the tears she could today.

"I'm alright. It's just been a long day."

That was an understatement, but she wasn't sure how else she could say it.

"You should clean up before Mother sees you," Anthony said slightly more rationally than his sister.

"Aunt Diana is here?" Thea asked.

Anthony shook his head.

"No. We've gotten rooms at the hotel and I sent word to my parents that we are staying here overnight."

Thea nodded, careful of her neck. "That would be nice. I didn't get much rest on the train."

Charlie let out a half-hysterical laugh. "I wouldn't have guessed. It's not as if someone tried to kill you."

Anthony wrapped one arm around his sister and the other around Thea and guided them both towards the exit.

Wilhelmina stood watching a porter in a red jacket load her luggage onto a trolley.

"I'll help you up, ma'am," she heard the porter say as he

noticed Wilhelmina swaying dangerously. The man guided Wilhelmina towards the lift.

"Was she one of the victim's family?" Charlie asked.

Thea shook her head gently. "The murderer tried to kill her. The doctor said she should be fine after some rest."

"That's good, at least." Charlie paled, as if realizing how callous that sounded. "I mean, it's good that she will be okay. It all sounds so horrible." The girl blinked, as if realizing something was out of place. "Where is your maid?"

"Molly was married to Mr. Talbot, the man who was killed. The police held her in York for questioning. She should be here in the morning."

Charlie paled further. "How horrible."

They moved towards the baggage car and directed a porter to gather Molly's and Thea's trunks. She was glad that the hotel was attached to the station.

They were in the lift before Thea spoke again. "I don't want to talk about it anymore. I just want to climb in a bed and sleep."

Anthony gave her a warm smile. "As soon as we get to the room," he promised.

She smiled at the thought. As soon as she got in her room, she was asleep before her head hit the pillow.

CHAPTER TWENTY-EIGHT

DESPITE NOT SLEEPING SOUNDLY, THEA DECIDED TO GET OUT OF bed early. Plagued by nightmares from the past few days, she had been unable to sleep longer and staying in bed just seemed pointless. The city was still rather asleep from the view she had from her window.

Being alone wasn't any better than trying to go back to sleep. Unable to take it anymore, she called one of the maids to draw her a bath. She soaked in leisure and rang for the girl to help her dress.

Thea was in no way ready to start her day, but the thought of being alone in her room a moment longer threatened to drive her mad.

That was how she found herself in the lift with James' jacket draped over her arm. She wasn't sure the man had even been at the hotel, let alone that he was still there.

"Ground floor," Thea told the attendant. He closed the doors and they started the descent when he stopped at one of the lower floors and opened the doors again. She studied the ironwork, unable to take staring at the doors or the attendant any longer.

"Ground floor?" a man asked the operator.

"Yes, sir."

Hearing James' voice, Thea looked up.

"Mr. Poyntz," she greeted, "What a coincidence. I have your jacket."

The man smiled at her as he took the garment from her. "Thank you, Lady Theodora."

"It was very kind of you to allow me to use it."

"No problem at all."

"I was going to head to the Palm Court for breakfast. Would you care to join me?" she offered. Thea hadn't thought when she first met the man that she would ever extend such an offer, but she didn't find herself retracting it. He was surprisingly pleasant company and she owed him her life.

James smiled and shook his head. "I appreciate the offer, but I'm afraid I have to be getting on. The news waits for no man."

She fought back an unladylike snort. James Poyntz was so much more than a newspaperman.

The lift came to a stop and the attendant opened up the doors. They stepped off and she turned to the man and reached for him to keep him from going. This might very well be the last time she saw him. How could she express what she felt, how much his kindness to a perfect stranger meant to her? Words seemed so inadequate.

"I can't possibly put into words how much I appreciate what you have done for me."

James shook his head and a charming smile replaced his serious façade once more. "It was nothing, Lady Theodora."

He looked like he might say something else but restrained himself.

"I suppose this is goodbye then."

Again, he shook his head. "No, not goodbye. We'll see each other again. So instead, I'll say au revoir, Lady Theodora."

"Au revoir, Mr. Poyntz," Thea replied, wondering why she felt comforted by the idea that they would meet again.

She offered him her hand and he squeezed it before he walked away. The look he gave her before he turned made Thea almost call out to him, to ask him what it was he wanted to say. Instead, she did what was proper and let him walk away.

———

THEA ENTERED THE OASIS THAT WAS THE PALM COURT, HOPING to find an empty table. Amongst its glittering glass dome and Venetian chandelier, she was pleasantly surprised to see Wilhelmina sitting alone at one of the tables, nursing a cup of coffee.

"Can I help you with something, my lady?" the host asked as she came closer. Thea shook her head.

"No. I found who I was looking for."

"Of course, my lady," the man bowed his head, allowing her to move into the court. Thea placed her hands on the back of the chair across from Wilhelmina.

"Is this seat taken?"

Wilhelmina jumped. She was still quite bleary-eyed as she looked up. "Oh, it's you, darling. Do sit."

Thea did just that. A waiter quickly filled a glass with water and came for her order. She relaxed in her chair as soon as he left.

"How are you doing this morning?"

"Terrible, nasty headache, I'm afraid," Wilhelmina muttered, glaring down at her cup of coffee. The dark liquid swirled in the delicate cup cradled between her trembling hands. It had a strong smell that wafted across the table. "The doctor said I was awfully lucky. All I needed was a few more sips and I wouldn't have woken up."

And then as if realizing just how morbid she had gotten, Wilhelmina straighten up and let out a long, deep sigh.

"Sorry. How are you doing?"

"Better." Thea subconsciously pressed her fingers to her throat. A moment longer and Mrs. Fletcher might have punctured it and she would have been dead too. The Woman had been insane, not caring about the trail of bodies in her wake. Thea was glad to be rid of her. "Honestly, I'm more grateful to have a bath and a change of clothes."

The American waved her hand dismissively. "I know exactly what you mean. The soak I had this morning was glorious. I might burn that suit. If I ever wear it again, it might be too soon."

Thea smiled at that. She clutched her hands together to keep from touching her throat again. Physically, she was perfectly fine. Playing with the spot the pin had pricked was only a matter of nervousness.

Thea forced her hands apart as the waiter brought back coffee and a Scottish breakfast. Her stomach turned at the sight of all the food. After her ordeal, it was barely appealing.

Her mother would have scolded her for playing with her food, Thea thought as she pushed the Lorne sausage and black pudding back and forth on the plate. The tattie scones were plain at least and not as hard on her stomach.

Thea reached for her coffee, not bothering to put any sugar or milk into the cup. The dark liquid was strong and boiling hot, far better than the tea they had served on the train. She hoped it would clear her head after the day she had had yesterday.

Wilhelmina's head perked up slightly as she looked at a point behind Thea.

"I do believe that's Constable Cooke there with your maid," the American started and Thea lifted her head, turning slightly.

Sure enough, there came Molly, dressed in a new set of mourning clothes. She had cleaned up and looked more like a lady and a widow. She wore a black suit and hat with minimal ornaments and little lace or trim. Tasteful and elegant.

Behind her, Constable Cooke escorted her to their table. He was dressed in a suit, a far cry from the ill-fitted uniform he had worn before.

They approached and Molly hesitated, but Thea offered her a small smile. Detective Constable Cooke pulled out the chair for her. Molly sat down in it, giving him a grateful smile.

"Allow me to re-introduce myself," Constable Cooke said, bowing slightly to them. "Detective Constable Cooke of the Metropolitan Police at your service, my lady, madam."

"Won't you sit?" Thea offered, motioning to the chair next to Molly. The man smiled but shook his head.

"Thank you, but I won't be staying long."

"Detective Constable?" Wilhelmina asked.

"I was assigned to investigate the Leeds City Police. There had been some reports of suspicious happenings in the station. I believe this was not the first case that Stanton tried to cover up." The constable glanced around the table. "I will be returning to London now that my work is done, though I figured that it was best I escort Mrs. Talbot here so no further incident might take place."

Thea had felt like something had been off about the man. The idea that he had been undercover made sense.

"Thank you for taking care of Molly," Thea told the constable. The man bowed his head. "Have a safe journey back to London."

"Thank you," he bowed his head. "Ladies."

With that, he turned and walked away. The three women were quiet for a short while, before the American woman predictably started up the conversation again.

"I'm terribly sorry for your loss. How are you doing?"

Wilhelmina turned to Molly. "You've been through a lot in the past few days."

Molly made a face. "I didn't realize how much Daniel was in my life. Now that he's gone, I don't think it's truly sunk in yet."

Thea reached her hand out to Molly, squeezing it in what she hoped would offer the other woman some support. What Molly had been through was horrific. The worst part was that Thea had no idea how she could help.

"Mr. Fletcher sent a telegram. It seems that we're now equal partners in Fletcher's, at least according to Daniel's will." She shifted, looking down at the coffee pot on the table as the waiter rushed over another cup. "Mr. Fletcher came up on business," Molly told them. "His family was from York. He was trying to get the money to repay his debts. Daniel had promised to let him run more of the business, if he could prove he was responsible. But to do that, Mr. Fletcher had to pay off the money he owed to his bookies."

Thea nodded. "That explains the return ticket. But what were the chances that Mrs. Fletcher decided to kill Mr. Talbot the same day that Mr. Fletcher was returning back to London?"

"Not very good," Molly admitted, "But Mrs. Fletcher would have known her husband's schedule. Mr. Fletcher was being very secretive about all this, but she would have known. He wanted to surprise Daniel for the two-year anniversary of their partnership. It must have been quite a shock to him to hear that Daniel was dead."

"I thought he was just an excellent actor," Inspector Thayne admitted sheepishly as he walked up to their table, having just entered the Palm Court. "I should have realized that anyone who owed that much money to bookies didn't have that good of a poker face."

The three women laughed at him and he gave that grin he had that first day on the train.

"Mr. Fletcher wants to continue to be business partners," Molly continued softly, "I told him that it would be the same arrangement as with my husband. He would have to quit gambling first. After spending years married to a murderess, he wasn't hesitant to repay his debts and give up gambling. He said his life had too much excitement in it to keep up the same lifestyle."

Thea stifled a laugh. Wilhelmina was not nearly as successful, laughing loudly enough to draw looks from the other tables. It was fortunate that the cafe was not very crowded yet.

"So what will you do now?" Wilhelmina asked in that blunt American way. "You're a woman of independent means. You can go anywhere, do anything. Do you truly plan to stay on at Fletcher's?"

Molly hesitated and Thea couldn't help the way her stomach dropped out. She had hoped that Molly didn't want to leave, but Thea also knew she couldn't reasonably expect that. Still, she would be lost without her help and friendship. Molly was irreplaceable.

Molly glanced at Thea but didn't speak. Inspector Thayne caught the look shared between the two of them and stood up suddenly.

"Mrs. Livingston, would you care to take a walk with me?"

Wilhelmina looked between the other two women and then stood as well, nodding. "I don't mind if I do, Inspector Thayne."

She took the inspector's arm and the two walked away, leaving Thea and Molly at the table.

CHAPTER TWENTY-NINE

"I'M SORRY THAT I'VE BEEN LYING TO YOU, MY LADY," MOLLY said dejectedly, glancing at her fingers on the table and back up at Thea.

Thea tried for what she hoped was a reassuring smile. Right now, the wrong word would go a long way to scare Molly off. "I understand why you did. I was hoping that you might stay on with me, but you don't need the money now, do you?"

The other woman's eyes got wide, the shock evident on her face. "Really? You're not angry with me?"

"Well, I had been when I first found out that you had lied, but I understand. Who's to say I wouldn't have done the same in your situation?" Thea reached out to the other woman, taking her hand so she would stop fiddling with her fingers. The movement was driving her insane, but Thea hoped Molly would interpret it as comforting. "So what will you do?"

"As much as I'd like to stay on as your companion, my lady," Molly hesitated, "it's not just me I have to think of anymore." Her hand rested protectively over her stomach. "Daniel left me a majority share of Fletcher's. I'm going back to London immediately to run the company. They're depending on me."

Thea couldn't help the wave of disappointment that came over her. She wanted to keep Molly close and in her life but reasonably knew that it wouldn't make sense for her to stay on as a maid.

"I will, however, help you find another maid," the young woman added.

"I appreciate that, Molly. Truly." Thea really did, but she was going to miss Molly.

"It's not like this is the last we'll see each other. We can see each other on the weekends. You'll come into Fletcher's. You'll like it. You'll be fine without me shadowing your every move, my lady."

Molly might be right about that. After all, she now had friends in Wilhelmina and Inspector Thayne. Molly would remain her friend as well, even if she was busy now running a company. Though Thea did wonder why she would have to wait for the 'weekends' to see Molly, whatever those were.

"Molly, you can call me 'Thea.' You don't work for me anymore."

Molly beamed a little, lighting up like sunshine and Thea couldn't help the grin that overtook her face.

THEA WAS FINISHING HER MEAL WHEN WILHELMINA AND Inspector Thayne sauntered back in. They looked perfectly comfortable with each other now, or at least, Inspector Thayne didn't look like he was doing everything he could to get away from her. Wilhelmina wasn't such terrible company once she'd toned down her overacting.

"Do you mind if we rejoin you?" Wilhelmina asked as they approached arm in arm. Thea felt a weird little twist in her chest seeing that, as if she couldn't quite swallow her coffee all the way. It was utterly peculiar.

"Not at all," Thea replied, forcing the now lukewarm liquid down anyway. "Though I was about to go back up to my room." Molly began to stand, but Thea shook her head. "Stay. Relax. Lord knows you need it."

Molly sat back down reluctantly, glancing between the other three. Inspector Thayne pulled out a chair for Wilhelmina and turned back to Thea, looking almost shy. "Would you mind if I walk you up?"

Thea glanced up at him as he offered his arm, a smile creeping over her face. "I was hoping you might ask."

THE RIDE IN THE LIFT WAS SURPRISINGLY COMFORTABLE. Inspector Thayne was standing beside her, almost a respectable distance from her, but if Thea were to reach out, she'd probably brush against his hand. The young man operating the lift kept his face away from them, more of a fixture than a person.

Thea glanced over at Inspector Thayne. His suit was plain but well-tailored and well made. The charcoal color emphasized the gray of his eyes. His tie was a mix of blue and grays. The chain of his pocket watch glinted out from where it was attached to his vest. It made him look handsome in a completely effortlessly way. He looked like the son of a baron, heading off to spend some time with his family. If she didn't know he was a policeman, she would have never suspected.

"I heard about what you did. I read the report," his voice a near whisper. "That was rather dangerous."

"Don't you mean rather stupid?" she asked him.

Inspector Thayne shook his head. "Lady Thea, the police exist for a reason. You have to trust that we'll do our jobs correctly."

"How could I, when there were those that were willing to cover up a murder? I couldn't let Molly be accused of something she didn't do."

He sighed heavily, eyes shut, before he turned and faced her. "I know. In the future though, should you wind up involved in any murders, please leave the crime-solving to the professionals." Thea pursed her lips. "Thea, promise me."

"Fine," she scowled, looking away. "I promise."

Inspector Thayne looked at her, reaching for her face. His hand was calloused but gentle against her cheek as he tipped her head up. "I want you to be safe. Is that a bad thing?"

Thea didn't answer. She didn't think it was, but the past day had been so overwhelming. She hated how it took being wrapped up in a murder investigation to make her feel alive. As much as she'd like to say that she'd leave anything that happened like this in the future to the police, she didn't want to. If she did, how could she ever feel this alive, this right, again?

Fortunately for her, Inspector Thayne couldn't read her mind. He didn't know that she felt that way.

When the lift stopped on her floor, Inspector Thayne offered her his arm again, returning to a more appropriate form of contact, and together they headed toward her room.

CHAPTER THIRTY

THEA PULLED HER KEY OUT WHEN THE DOOR SWUNG OPEN FROM the inside, revealing Anthony. He must have come through the adjoining doors to direct the staff which of her cases they should take.

"I was just about to come down to look for you," her cousin said before he spotted Inspector Thayne. "Who's this?"

Her checks were warm. She hoped Inspector Thayne wasn't looking at her.

"This is the Honorable Leslie Thayne." She swallowed, moistening her lips. "Detective Inspector Thayne." Thea lifted her eyes slightly, risking a glance at Inspector Thayne. "Inspector, this is my cousin, Lord Auldkirk."

Anthony offered his hand to Inspector Thayne. "I have to thank you, Inspector, for looking after my cousin on the trip."

"I'm afraid I can't take all the credit."

Thea was sure she was blushing now. It was more out of embarrassment than anything else. She hated all eyes being on her like this.

"Well then, I guess I can go back inside, since you've been

found now." Anthony was two seconds away from laughing. His eyes were full of mirth, barely contained. "Carry on."

As he turned away, he was chuckling loudly.

"Subtle," Thea muttered under her breath.

"Very," Inspector Thayne replied dryly.

He glanced towards the interior of the room, watching Anthony and Charlie. It seemed in her absence, her cousins had taken up residence in her room.

"I suppose this is where we part," Inspector Thayne said softly. "I'm leaving now."

Thea swallowed her disappointment at that. She didn't like the idea that she was never going to see him again. An idea struck her suddenly and she pulled her purse open, digging through until she found one of her calling cards. "This is my address in London. If you wanted to meet again."

He smiled at her, taking the card in his hands and turning it over a few times, running his fingers over the embossed letters. "And what about while you're here in Scotland?"

"One moment," she said, stepping inside the room and up to her cousins, "Do you have a card?"

Charlie's brow furrowed slightly, but she reached inside her purse and gave Thea one without argument. She returned to the inspector's side, holding it out to him. He took it and placed it with the other.

"I hope to see you soon, Inspector."

He lifted her hand to his lips, giving her that charming smile once more. Shivers ran up her arm. His lips felt smooth on the back of her hand even through her gloves and she could almost imagine them on her own, flushing at the thought. "Until we meet again, Lady Thea."

Thea smiled, remaining there in the hallway, watching Inspector Thayne's retreating form.

"So who was that?" Charlie batted her eyelashes and giggled. "He was handsome."

Thea glared but otherwise didn't feel like dignifying that with a response. Sometimes it was hard to remember that Charlie was only a few years younger than her. Instead, Thea moved to finish packing.

"I think, little sister, that our dear cousin has a beau." Thea's cheeks felt heated from Anthony's teasing words, despite the fact that they weren't true. She wanted them to be true.

"I only just met him the day before yesterday on the train," Thea snapped.

"But you want to see him again." She blushed deeper and ducked her head. Charlie laughed a little louder.

"Let's just get going. We need to find Molly and I should say goodbye to Wilhelmina."

"Who's Wilhelmina?" Anthony teased as he waited for the porters to pick up their trunks. "Is she another of your new mysterious friends you met on this train?"

"I wouldn't quite use the word 'friend,'" Thea sighed, "Not yet. Acquaintance, perhaps. We did meet on the train. I think you'd like her."

Anthony would really like Wilhelmina, Thea thought. They had the same sort of ostentatious nature about them. There was a sort of vibrance to them, a hypnotic nature that drew others to them while simultaneously repulsing them. It was unfortunate that Wilhelmina was married and thus made her an unsuitable contender for being a viscountess. Wilhelmina would have been a far more acceptable addition to her family than whatever harpy would sink her claws into her cousin.

THE RIDE DOWN TO THE LOBBY WAS RELATIVELY QUIET. IT WAS only that way because neither Anthony nor Charlie had much experience being silent. Thea supposed that when you were in a large boisterous family and had to fight to have your voice heard, the motto of 'seen and not heard' didn't exactly apply. Where she and Cecil had both been quiet children, their cousins had never known the meaning of the word.

Still, Thea was surprised they went the entire ride down without asking her once if she was alright or if Inspector Thayne was a suitor. The two of them had already shared laughter over that idea at her expense when they had been in the room. Thea had to bite her tongue to keep from replying and now was just happy to tune them out.

The attendant opened the door as he stopped the lift. The lobby bustled with people, but after the last two days, Thea was almost ready for the peace and quiet of the Scottish countryside.

Wilhelmina stood chatting with Molly.

"I'll be back," Thea told her cousins. She walked in their direction, ignoring whatever reaction her cousins were having. She knew it was out of character for her. She never had very many friends, had never strayed outside of her small social circle. It must have been a shock to her cousins that she had met so many people.

"Inspector Thayne just said goodbye," Wilhelmina said.

Thea fought the urge to blush. She could feel the heat rushing up to them despite her efforts. The two of them continued talking like she wasn't even there.

"He's a good man," Molly said solemnly, looking every bit the part of the mourning widow.

"He is indeed," Wilhelmina agreed. "And a good looking one too."

At this point, Thea could no longer stop the blush that rose to her cheeks and she glanced away. She did not want to discuss with anyone whether or not she thought Mr. Thayne was a good-looking man. The other woman, sensing her embarrassment, laughed loudly.

"I do think I'll miss you," Wilhelmina said, candid as always, her voice taking on a softer, quieter quality to it.

Despite everything, Thea found that she would miss her too. Wilhelmina had brought out a side of her she hadn't known existed, one that craved adventure and excitement.

"And I you. Here is my card. We should get together for lunch sometime in London."

Wilhelmina smiled at her, brightly and genuinely.

"That would be lovely."

Anthony and Charlotte were waiting for her by the door to the street. They looked like quite the pair. Anthony, for all his good looks, was dressed like he was double his age. His sister on the other hand was rather plain looking, but Charlie made up for it with her fashionable clothes and bubbly personality.

Anthony was handsome as he was brilliant. There was a delicate structure to his face, a classical beauty to him. And Wilhelmina had clearly noticed. She was staring right at him.

"Are you alright?" Thea asked the other woman, acting as if she hadn't seen the same thing happen with countless other women. The reactions were hardly surprising after the few misadventures she had gone on with her cousins when they had been together. Anthony was a gorgeous man and it seemed as if every woman he encountered seemed to fall madly in love with him.

Anthony smiled, seeing Wilhelmina staring, and lifted a hand in greeting. Almost shyly, Wilhelmina lifted a hand to return the wave, a blush spreading across her cheeks.

"Who is that?" Wilhelmina asked softly.

"My cousins, Anthony and Charlotte." Thea smiled and waved back, feeling a little cheeky. It felt nice to get a bit of her own back.

Molly was trying to hide a smile. She too had been a witness to this unfortunate occurrence that happened to women of all ages. Though now Thea understood why Molly had never been one of those to fall madly in love with him.

"You do realize just how handsome he is, don't you?" Wilhelmina asked, sounding back to her old self, like she had when Thea had first met her. "Perhaps we might arrange something while we're both in Scotland. You would bring your cousins, of course."

Thea laughed and Molly giggled behind her hand. The only thing that would improve the situation would be if Anthony and Charlie were to come over. To have them see Wilhelmina's reaction would make up for their earlier teasing.

"Of course," Thea said. She gave Wilhelmina a smile and the American woman reached out, pulling her close, then repeated the action with Molly. Molly's expression was as shocked as Thea felt, wide eyed but otherwise showing nothing. "I'll see you both soon."

She decided to take a page out of Wilhelmina's book and hugged Molly quickly, before turning and joining her cousins. The three of them headed outside to their automobile. If Thea tried not to think too hard about it, everything would be like it had been. It was hard to believe that a mere few days ago, Thea had only been going to visit her cousins. There had been nothing remotely interesting about her life.

Now, that was hardly true. Her life would never be boring again, Thea realized as she sat in the Rolls-Royce Landaulette. It felt like the world around her was in color for the first time, like she had been living her life with her eyes closed until now.

The automobile's exterior was a cherry red, but the buttery leather interior was the color of honey. It made it almost ironic that such a colorful automobile was called a Silver Ghost.

"Good morning, Donald," Thea greeted the chauffeur. He had only worked for her cousins' for the last few years.

He bowed his head.

"Good morning, my lady." He reached for the last piece of

luggage on the trolley. "I am sorry to hear about your ordeal, my lady, and glad to hear you are unharmed."

She smiled at him. "Thank you."

Donald ducked his head, opening the door for them. She climbed in and her cousins followed. Donald closed the door firmly behind them and ran to get in. It was only then that they were finally on their way north to Ravenholm Castle.

CHAPTER THIRTY-ONE

THEA WAS LOOKING FORWARD TO TAKING A HOT BATH AND having a good meal before she climbed into a warm bed when they reached Ravenholm Castle. Located along one of the many Scottish lochs, the castle boasted uninterrupted views of the water and village on the other side, the one that the castle was named for.

One of the grand, ornate doors opened for them as the automobile stopped in front of the entrance. The butler, Mr. Semple, was waiting for them.

"My lord, my ladies," the butler greeted them as they walked inside. "This arrived for Lady Theodora."

He presented her a letter and letter opener on a silver tray. Inside, there was a short note.

To Lady Theodora, a most exceptional woman-
This article and photograph will be printed in the Thursday
evening edition of the West End Gazette.
J.P.

Thea plucked the note off, revealing a freshly typed copy of the promised article. A picture of her as the Edinburgh police escorted Mrs. Fletcher away was tucked in the envelope as well.

MURDER ON THE FLYING SCOTSMAN
By James Poyntz

EDINBURGH - Thursday saw the arrest of Mildred Stanton Fletcher, wife of famed department store owner Lionel Fletcher, and her father Detective Inspector Louis Stanton. Mrs. Fletcher has been apprehended on charges of the murder of Daniel Talbot, co-owner of Fletcher's. Detective Chief Inspector Stanton of the Leeds City Police was taken into custody after the discovery that he had concealed evidence in the investigation.

FRAMED - Miss Margaret Forbes, companion of Lady Theodora Prescott-Pryce, was accused of the murder and arrested on Tuesday afternoon in York. On Wednesday, Mr. Fletcher was also arrested in London upon suspicion of Talbot's murder. Both acquainted with the deceased, Stanton and Mrs. Fletcher sought to use Miss Forbes and Mr. Fletcher as scapegoats for Mrs. Fletcher's actions. Miss Forbes and Mr. Fletcher have since been released.

Lady Theodora worked with Metropolitan Police Detective Inspector Leslie Thayne to solve the crime. Under her prompting, they cleared Miss Forbes' and Mr. Fletcher's names. Inspector Thayne was traveling to visit his family at their estate in Scotland at the time of the murder. Acting with exemplary character, Inspector Thayne is set to be recognized by Miss Forbes' family upon his return to London.

According to other passengers on the train, Lady Theodora exhibited commendable bravery, facing and restraining Mrs. Fletcher until police arrived in Edinburgh to arrest her. Because of her actions, a murderer and a corrupt policeman are behind bars and two innocent people walk free.

Thea lowered the article, smiling as she did so.

"What is it?" Charlie asked, trying her best to read over Thea's shoulder. "Is it from someone exciting?"

"Better yet, sister dear," Anthony said as he plucked the paper from her hands. "It seems our little cousin is going to be a published crime fighter."

"A what?" the other girl asked, her eyes going wide.

"Mhmm," he hummed as he read the article. "It seems little Thea's had quite the adventure on the train ride here. She caught a murderer, uncovered a police scandal, and cleared a few innocent people."

Charlie leaned on her brother's arm, looking down at the article.

"Well," she huffed, looking at Thea, "I guess if I want to have any adventures, I'll have to stick with you."

Thea couldn't hold it back any longer, not between the seriousness of Anthony's expression or the outraged one on Charlie's face. She laughed.

ALSO SET IN THEA'S WORLD:

Lady Thea Mystery

Book 1: Murder on the Flying Scotsman

Book 1.5: The Unread Letter

Book 2: The Corpse at Ravenholm Castle

Book 3: A Most Fashionable Murder

———————

An Invitation to Tea: A Historical Romance Novella

A NOTE TO THE READERS

Dear Readers,

If you enjoyed this book, please consider leaving a review.

This book has been edited and proofread. However, authors and editors are not infallible, so if you find errors, please contact me at the social media links below or contact@jessicabakerauthor.com.

Thank you.

facebook.com/jessicabakerauthor

twitter.com/JCBakerAuthor

instagram.com/jessicabakerauthor

ABOUT THE AUTHOR

Named for the famous fictional mystery writer Jessica Fletcher, Jessica Baker picked up a pen when she was in elementary school and never set it down.

Jessica lives in sunny Central Florida and is a member of the National Sisters in Crime. When she's not writing, she works at a university and freelances as a camera assistant in film which provides plenty of inspiration for her stories.

To learn more about Jessica and her books, visit her at www.jessicabakerauthor.com and for the latest information, subscribe to her newsletters.

Printed in Great Britain
by Amazon